Tommy

SIMON CORRIGAN

Tommy Was Here

An *Abacus* Book

First published in Great Britain in 1992 by André Deutsch
This edition published in 1993 by Abacus

Copyright © 1992 by Simon Corrigan

The moral right of the author has been asserted.

*All characters in this publication are fictitious
and any resemblance to real persons, living or dead,
is purely coincidental.*

All rights reserved.
No part of this publication may be reproduced,
stored in a retrieval system, or transmitted, in any
form or by any means without the prior
permission in writing of the publisher, nor be
otherwise circulated in any form of binding or
cover other than that in which it is published
and without a similar condition including this
condition being imposed on the subsequent purchaser.

A CIP catalogue record for this book
is available from the British Library.

ISBN 0 349 10555 3

Printed in England by Clays Ltd, St Ives plc

Abacus
A Division of
Little, Brown and Company (UK) Limited
165 Great Dover Street
London SE1 4YA

To Klára Tóth

An artist is originally a man who turns away from reality because he cannot come to terms with the renunciation of instinctual satisfaction which it at first demands, and who allows his erotic and ambitious wishes full play in the life of fantasy. He finds a way back to reality, however, from his world of fantasy by making use of special gifts to mould his fantasies into truths of a new kind, which are valued by men as precious reflections of reality. Thus in a certain fashion, he actually becomes the hero, the king, the creator, or the favourite he desired to be, without following the long roundabout path of making alterations in the external world. But he can only achieve this because other men feel the same dissatisfaction that he does . . . and because that dissatisfaction . . . is itself a part of reality.

Freud: 'Formulations on the Two Principles of Moral Functioning'

And then she'll be sorry

She will take a taxi from the airport, will give the name and address of the hotel, then, when the driver irritably refuses to understand her English French, will hand him the piece of paper: *Hotel Berlioz, Passage Jouffroy, Paris 9ème*. It will be her first defeat. She will give him too large a tip, will shake away his offers – half-hearted anyway – of help with her luggage, will proceed up the passageway alone, looking neither right nor left at the overflowing stalls of antiquarian-book dealers or at the opulence of seafoods from the fishing villages of Brittany now banked on tiers of crushed ice in the lustrous window of the brasserie.

The hotel, at the end of its *belle époque* passage, is modest and inexpensive: a precaution, since she doesn't know how long she will be staying. She has booked for a preliminary three nights, to be prolonged as necessary. And yet it is not impossible, or so she tells herself, that tomorrow evening she will be back in England, laughing at her extravagant folly and able in her relief even to smile across at her aged husband, long recipient only of her derision or indifference, as he sits eternally gripping the arms of his chair as if the better to sustain the weight of his years and disappointments. It is not impossible to believe that her panic is groundless and Thomas safe, not kidnapped nor lost in drugs, but on holiday or living with a girl or someone, or else ill but recovering.

It is warmer in Paris than in London. She stands for a moment in the lobby, like a high and perspiring statue, then sets down her bags, wipes her forehead with the back of her hand, and approaches the desk: 'Do you speak English?' By way of reply the girl appears to address an invisible third party: 'Ah, the English lady.' Imogen signs a register and pays her three nights in advance as arranged with the unpleasant travel agent in Petersfield who twice asked her, unnecessarily and as if demanding some kind of recompense for his having secured her a flight and a room at such short notice, what it was she planned to do in Paris. The girl hands her a key. '. . . No, I'll manage my own luggage, thank you.' So this is Paris, this hotel lobby's shabby elegance, the hectic bazaar of the boulevard outside, this the city where Thomas has lived and studied for two years without her having visited him or even paused to formulate a picture of his life there. She asks: 'Do you know where it is, the rue du Faubourg Saint-Denis?'

'But certainly,' says the girl, very small, very neat. 'It is not far from here. You wish to go there?'

'My son,' says Imogen, 'lives in the rue du Faubourg Saint-Denis.' The receptionist, as one too young to feel any empathetic maternal glow, gives a perfunctory smile. Then the smile fades slightly, her eyes slither over the lobby as if Imogen's son might have somehow materialised there. 'Your son, he does not know you are here, in Paris?'

'No, not yet,' says Imogen. 'It's a surprise.'

'Of course, yes,' says the receptionist. She disapproves, thinks Imogen: to her I am an interfering, a spying mother. Mothers do not arrive, unannounced, to surprise their sons enjoying the fruits of this city of wicked repute. 'Of course, a surprise. He will be very happy. You wish to know how to go there? You wish to go immediately?'

Imogen's room is dark, the net curtains are old and not altogether clean. She looks hard at the double bed – no single rooms are, alas, available, you understand, at this time of year – and at the long forbidding bolster, a relic from another era. She flicks on the light of the tiny bathroom, flicks it off, then returns to lay out her dresses and skirts on the bed, not even crossing to the window, that instinctive gesture by which we take possession of each new dwelling-place, however long or short the stay.

Only once before has he given her real cause for alarm. In his lower sixth year he took an overdose of sleeping pills and was taken to hospital. There was no more than a moment of danger, for it transpired that the overdose was not so great and that the pills in question, even if ingested in huge quantities, rarely proved fatal. But Tommy was at a boarding school in the North and by this time Imogen, woken shortly after midnight by the housemaster's call, was driving through the rainy Midlands, her eyes fixed on the road which unwound mercilessly before her beyond the swimming windscreen and far on into the treacherous gradients of the Pennines. When she arrived at the hospital Thomas had already been stomach-pumped and lay sleeping. She caved in with relief and delayed shock and was given a sturdy brandy, then driven to the school by the headmaster who offered her a bed in the sick bay, the only accommodation, he regretted, available. It was seven o'clock already and the school was stirring; the children, some still in pyjamas, others already in full uniform, watched from the windows as she crossed the courtyard with her unmistakable and heroic stride. Some of them, friends of Thomas or acquaintances, recognised her from parties or school functions or holidays when Thomas had invited them to stay. In the sick bay she was persuaded to take a tranquilliser and try to get some sleep only after repeated assurances that she would be woken at the least news from the hospital.

A few hours later, sitting there undaunted on the school sickroom bed, she was able to view the disaster with some sort of perspective. She went over the night's events, that telephone call, the nightmare drive and the sorcerous weather, the hospital and its stunning, indelicate fluorescents. But try as she might she could not imagine what was to follow, could not envisage what she would do when Thomas awoke, what she would say to him, how she would touch him, drive him home or leave him there, fetch him delicate convalescent lunches in bed or write him letters of firm and patient reassurance.

In the restaurant with the headmaster she was anxious above all to know if Thomas would have to leave the school, that very famous and expensive school into which she had poured so much money and which surpassed in prestige even the great public schools of the South, since talent – specifically musical talent – was the ultimate, the only real criterion for entry, and this, as she would often say, was something that could not be bought. The headmaster assured her that no, in the circumstances it wouldn't be necessary. Tommy was not the first: cases like this were an occupational hazard in his school, where two hundred precociously gifted, high-strung and sensation-seeking adolescents dwelt in tight and jealous proximity. 'They're bored, they want attention, so they swallow a few aspirin, they make a few scratches with a Bic . . .'

What surprised him, he explained, was that Thomas had never belonged to this set, the posturing and self-styled *enfants terribles*. All this he related as Imogen sat, pushing her fork about her plate, too rigid to eat, her remarkable eyes fixed on him. She felt she should furnish some defence of Thomas. The headmaster coughed and asked if it were true that she was divorcing her husband. Divorcing . . . ? Why yes, Thomas had given his housemaster to understand . . . surely that was why he had been so depressed of late? And so for the first time she heard the details of domestic atrocity given out by Thomas over the last months to staff and pupils alike, the allegations of terrible scenes, threats, adulteries. Realising that her loyalty remained with Thomas even as he betrayed and slandered her, she began at once to weave a scenario that would accord with his own, wherein no, they hadn't given Tommy a particularly happy home life, nor been ideal parents for all their open-handedness. She said: 'Well, of course, as you said just now, these children are inclined to exaggerate. I and my husband have our problems, like anyone else. I had no idea Tommy was so affected . . .'

And so she continued, exonerating Thomas from his morass of deceptions by heaping the blame on herself. The headmaster did not believe her; she knew he would have liked to expel Thomas, rid himself of this rich, troubling, rather brilliant and aloof pupil who contrived to wear the school uniform as if he were slumming and was polite to his teachers as if it demanded too much effort to be otherwise.

She went to the hospital, where Thomas still drifted in and out of sleep. She concentrated on his face, his stirrings, his fluttering eyelids, and in this way could almost forget that he was recovering from something more than a bad case of 'flu or fever. With his crumpled pyjamas and his hair, rather too long, tousled among the pillows and into his eyes, he looked very touching. And she decided, with what she took for a sudden great access of tact and magnanimity, to refer to the whole business only if and when Thomas himself was ready to speak about it. This resolved, she was already able to look at his wondrous sleeping face more warmly and tenderly. She sat there, her eyes filled with gratifying tears, until Thomas shifted, blinked, sighed, lifted his head from the pillow, and smiled at her with that smile of his, all the more sincere in that it flowered out of this deep and so near-fatal sleep, was given to anyone, free of charge, vacant, guileless, destined solely to disarm.

She sets herself before the desk and gestures to the payphone in the lobby. 'I can use this?'

'Yes, of course,' says the girl. 'Do you have some French money?'

The telephone is set in its recess but there is no door, no means of shutting herself off from the receptionist who without even wanting to will hear the desolating silence of Thomas's absence. Imogen tries the number three times before realising that she is distractedly adding the code for Paris. Finally she hears the ringing of his phone as she heard it on three consecutive Sunday afternoons at the appointed time, then in the middle of the week and every other day after that, then ringing each day at all hours, late into the night or in the early morning and at odd times when she felt she might conceivably catch him at home. Very much aware of the girl at the desk with her paperback, Imogen turns her back to the lobby and counts the rings. Before, he would answer on the second or third. Imogen hangs up; the receptionist remains apparently absorbed in her novel. Imogen takes out Daniel's number and dials. A girl answers in French.

'Hello, I'm looking for Daniel Solomon. Is he there, please?'

Daniel comes to the phone, is surprised to hear from her and rather brusque. 'No, I haven't seen Thomas for a couple of months. No, I really have no idea where he might be.' She feels embarrassed: the over-anxious mother. 'But, you know,' says Daniel in his new and faintly transatlantic drawl, 'Thomas and I don't see too much of each other these days.'

'Well, yes, of course, I see. It's just that his phone isn't answering. Well, perhaps it's nothing. But Daniel —'

'Yes?'

'There was a postcard too. Oh, it's too complicated to explain over the phone. Daniel: do you think we can meet?'

'*Meet*? But where? When?'

'Now. I mean this evening. If you can. If you could.'

'I'm sorry, now, but . . . where exactly *are* you?'

'Hotel Berlioz, Passage Jouffroy. I don't know the name of the – I don't know Paris at all, you see.' Then she realises: of course, Daniel can have no idea that she is in France, must have thought her safely at home in Haslemere in the house he used to visit six, eight years ago.

'Now I'm with you. Well, yes, then I guess we must meet. Of course.' His voice is thoughtful and unenthusiastic. They make an appointment for seven in the large brasserie on the boulevard, just alongside the passage.

'Of course, I'll treat you,' she adds hurriedly.

'It's not that,' says Daniel, 'it's just that Renata – that's my girlfriend – and I were —'

'Oh, and of course, she must come too.'

Now it is time to go off in search of Thomas, go at least to the place where Thomas lives. She crosses the lobby without looking up and is almost at the door when 'Have you managed to speak with your son?' calls out the girl with hypocritical enthusiasm. 'No. No, I haven't,' Imogen says.

She married young, and disastrously, having thrown up a scholarship at the Royal College of Art in frustration at the antiquated strictures of her professors. It was at this time that the young David Hockney was a rising star, and in her letter to the Directorship, aside from a liberal smearing of words such as 'imbecilic', 'ineptitude', 'fossilised', 'dinosaur', she demanded what respect she owed to a teaching staff who 'went into drooling panegyrics over a boy who tears up Underground posters and calls it Art'. She also said she would repay 'every last penny' of her scholarship, an offer which fortunately the college did not take up and which she would have had considerable difficulty in fulfilling. Her first husband, an art dealer, a chauvinist and a snob, intended to trawl her in his magnificent wake as a decorative appendage through the salons of his social progress. She was seduced by his continued eloquence on the World of Art, for he was a great talker. It was only after she heard this same eloquence cranked out word for word at a dozen openings and a dozen receptions that she began to have doubts as to the substance beneath. In any case she could never have been anyone's escort or accomplice, for already she was too outspoken and too unversed in hyprocrisy to tolerate his mediocre and tedious acquaintances. At a private viewing she trenchantly criticised the artist's work within the woman's hearing – unknowingly, for she was incapable of cruelty – and by this characteristic folly cost her husband two years' judicious social manoeuvring. On learning her mistake she was so devastated that she dispatched a series of abject letters to the insulted artist which only succeeded in offending her further. It was the end of the marriage. In her shaken and penniless pride she took her two children, then aged four and six, to sleep for an entire summer on the floor of a Czech painter friend's Chelsea studio. She accepted all manner of temporary employment to provide for her children in their straitened circumstances, insatiably determined to atone for making them fatherless. And when in time she found herself timidly courted by a widowed farmer some thirty years her senior, a charming and ineffectual gentleman of means who had come upon Imogen one morning hauling easels and paintboxes doggedly over the deluged cart-tracks of his land and who had developed an immediate and melancholy affection for the trespasser, it was for the children that she accepted him and accepted the renunciation which the marriage entailed.

She moved into and took over his large house near Haslemere. She was introduced to his son and daughter, only a few years younger than herself. They saw her as an adventuress and so she came to feel, swiftly appalled at the loveless alacrity with which she had married him and brought her two demi-orphans under his roof. Used only to London, she set about adapting to wealthy country life. She cemented the marriage with two more sons a dutiful year apart. She entertained his bridge friends and hung her paintings and the paintings of her own friends and mentors on the walls of his house. She employed every ounce of her considerable and hitherto neglected charm to win acceptance and even admiration from a society she despised and secretly derided. The practice of her art, for which she had once been ready to sacrifice everything, was relegated to tiny islands of solitude, a month here, a fortnight there, as her husband grew older and more dependent, and her children older and more demanding. Soon it was quite normal for her to be up at dawn to do Thomas's packing and then drive him and his brother up to London, Thomas to his college lodgings and Damien to his 'cello lesson, throughout which she would wait in a corner café, then back to Haslemere with Damien to pick up her youngest, Toby, drive him up to school in Manchester to arrive at seven in the evening, attending a parents' evening and passing the night in a hotel before rising once more at dawn to drive back to Haslemere and prepare the house for Vicky, her daughter, who was coming down from London for a few days with her boyfriend. During termtime, when there were no concerts to attend in the various farflung schools, no birthday parties to arrange, no weekends when one or other of her children felt the need to come home and be fed and pampered, when her husband was not ill with the afflictions and depressions attendant on his great age, then she was able to drive off again to the cottage in Wales to paint, harried by urgency, counting the too few brief days that remained to her and as often as not called home prematurely by some illness or crisis in the family, for her husband resented these absences, and the temperamental Toby had frequent problems at school.

A few months previously Thomas had acquired an answering machine, and sometimes when Imogen made her Sunday calls it was not Thomas's voice she heard but a few bars from some overwrought German symphony and then a girl speaking in French. Usually Thomas called her back within a few hours. 'Who's the girl?' she asked once. He laughed – 'Oh, that!' – and carried on talking about something else. In a sense she lived for these Sunday calls although there was nothing very extraordinary about them, she making the standard half-serious complaints against the rest of the family while Tommy fed her anodyne snippets of news, reassuring her with his calm, smiling voice that he was fine, everything was fine. In the middle of the week sometimes, in her insomniac loneliness, she sat at the big kitchen table and scribbled off long letters to him, pages and pages about her infernal marriage, her losing battle with her painting, her fear of failure and dire need for his success. They never referred to these letters on the phone. Sometimes again, when she called, she had the impression that someone else was there with Thomas, as indeed why should there not be? But again she never asked, nor did Thomas volunteer the information.

It was on these tacitly agreed terms of mutual misunderstanding that they conducted their relationship through the first year and a half of Thomas's stay in Paris, until the Sunday when Imogen called up and there was nothing, not even an answering machine. She assumed it was broken or that Thomas had forgotten to turn it on before going away for the weekend, as it seemed he sometimes did, having friends with families in the country. She had other concerns at the time and did not try to reach him again until the following Sunday. Once again there was no reply of any kind. Her capacity for worry was capricious and depended on all kinds of external and unrelated factors. The following Sunday, unaccountably, she panicked, calling at four o'clock and then at roughly half-hour intervals late into the night. Her daughter, at home for a few days, succeeded in calming her down, but as soon as Vicky left on Wednesday morning Imogen became hysterical, rattling the receiver, shouting at her husband when he entered the room as if he, by some obscure oversight, were to blame. During the next few days she tried Thomas's number at least fifty times.

And then there was the postcard from Susan: 'I'm in Paris now! Just needed a break now that the twins are back at school. It's changed since the last time I was here – twenty years ago! By the way, I'd only been here a few hours and I saw Thomas in the street! He looked very different. We didn't talk – he was with someone and seemed busy, and I don't think he noticed me. I thought I'd drop you a line anyway. Ring me or . . .'

She called Susan straight away, and there was no answer. She looked at the postmark: the card had taken a week to arrive. Imogen calculated that at the outside Susan must have seen Thomas two weeks before. And Thomas had not called or answered for four and a half weeks now.

Who had he been with when Susan saw him? A girl, a man? Why did he seem *busy*, in what way *different*? Did she mean ill? Perhaps he had been ill. Ill, or drugged? Would Susan know the difference? Did

Thomas take drugs? And at once a thousand possibilities crowded out from behind Susan's words. A man, a woman? What business were they about? What had Thomas ever done to make her think he might take drugs?

'Oh, it's you, Imogen. How are you? . . . You got my postcard, well, yes, don't mention it. Well, I was carrying it around for days, you know me. It was seeing Thomas like that that made me think of writing it. Yes, the first day, it must have been, let me see, the fourteenth. What did I mean by *what*? Oh, did I write that?' There was a silence. 'Oh well, I don't know, I suppose I meant that I haven't seen him for ages, and these young people grow up so quickly, don't they. Suddenly you see them and it's a new hairstyle, new clothes . . .'

Susan had seen Thomas only four months before, at Imogen's New Year's Day party.

'Anyway, don't give it another thought, I couldn't even swear it was him. I'm sure he's doing splendidly. Listen, it's wonderful to hear from you. I was actually just on my way out. Maybe if I called you back sometime, when I have more time? And for God's sake don't go worrying your head about Tommy.' She laughed. 'I'm sure he's managing very well down there in the wicked city.'

It was then, in the silence which followed, that Imogen made up her mind to go to Paris. That afternoon she booked her flight, booked herself a hotel room. Suddenly exhausted, she fell asleep in an armchair after dinner, and was dragged awake long after eleven by the telephone and Susan.

'I'm sorry, I've been feeling dreadful since I spoke to you. You'll think I'm an idiot. But when you said you hadn't heard from him in weeks I just began to feel so guilty. I don't know why I didn't just tell you the truth there and then. You see, it was just a *feeling.*' Susan was crying now. 'It wasn't in the street that I saw him, at all. At least, not really. He was sitting in a café, in the window. And I just stood there, you know, amazed at the coincidence, and wondering if I should go in and say hello to him. And the next thing, he was standing on the pavement, there was a big car there. And he was talking through the window to somebody – the driver, I suppose – and then he got inside, and the car drove off. That's all. I'm sorry.'

The most important thing, Imogen told herself, is to stop Susan crying. If I can do that why then the whole thing will not seem so awful. Imogen said: 'Don't worry, don't worry. Did he look ill?'

'No, no. He looked in the pink of health. I only saw him for a moment. He looked better than I've ever seen him.'

'And this car? This person?'

Susan said: 'Really, I'm sorry, I don't know anything. I just wanted to tell you. I don't know why I wrote what I did. I don't know why I didn't tell you this afternoon. I'm sorry.'

As she lay in bed that night she had in her mind an image of her son coming out into the street, leaning over to speak through the open window, stepping into the car. He would be standing on some elegant Parisian avenue of perfume shops and jewellery shops. It is midday. The car is long, sleek, black, expensive. Tommy is wearing a big loose white shirt and jeans. But the expression on his face, even the set of his features, she cannot picture to herself. Is he smiling? She knows his hair is brown and thick: but the exact brown of his hair she cannot recall. She knows his eyes are dark and long-lashed: but their colour and light escape her. She cannot remember what her son looks like. And the memories of the past years, Tommy at all ages, the holidays, the illnesses, the celebrations, decompose and disperse, as dusty and devoid of meaning as old facts learnt in school, until Thomas is and will only ever be this figure in someone else's account: a stranger glimpsed on a city pavement, standing in some historical relation to her and yet quite unfamiliar, receding, irretrievable, watching with intimate knowledge and confidence the foreign street for a moment before climbing into someone else's car.

The wicked city

Imogen takes the metro to Strasbourg Saint-Denis, Tommy's ill-famed *quartier*. The receptionist said: 'It's very easy to find, this street. You only have to walk out of the metro exit and there it is.' But there seem to be a dozen metro exits, each one grubbier, more vile-smelling than the last, and signs directing her to at least half a dozen different streets. Along the platform black men are sitting, some in jeans and T-shirts, others in immaculate dark suits and impossibly white shirts. They make no move to board the train. One boy is playing a set of African drums, very loud. A drunk lies across two plastic seats. Imogen moves with the crowd, up one escalator, then another, then through a set of automatic gates. The station is very crowded, with many young North

Africans and West Indians. Some boys jump over the barrier without buying a ticket; as Imogen watches, two policemen close in on them from the shadows. A woman pushes her out of the way with an exaggerated sigh of impatience. Imogen walks past various station boutiques selling belts, costume jewellery, blank cassettes, hair products. Young black women sit behind the counter, indifferent in the underworld light. The passageway smells of urine. Ahead of her she sees a blue sign – RUE DU FAUBOURG SAINT-DENIS. All across the lower staircase sit a group of adolescents dressed up as punks. Their clothes are black, their hair either jet-black or white-blond. Other travellers step aside them with practised distaste and it is Imogen, in her coat too warm for the Paris spring and too elegant for this district, that they fasten on, shifting closer together so she cannot pass. Correctly assuming that they want money, she fixes her eyes on her feet and shakes her head. Apathetically they let her through, throw some half-hearted abuse after her.

She stands at the busy intersection of the Grand Boulevard and of rues Saint-Denis and Faubourg Saint-Denis. Around her are cheap boutiques, fast-food shops, pavement cafés, kebab houses, butchers' shops, sex shops, fruit stalls, wholesale garment outlets. Men in shirtsleeves manoeuvre racks of dresses between prostitutes who smoke and chat in the gateways to stinking and dilapidated courtyards where fearful old residents watch from behind blinds as pimps transact with drug-pedlars in stairwells or calculate the comings and goings of the girls. Youngsters are gathered around the entrances to the metro or perched on railings; they pass round cigarettes and watch the harried street in their vast boredom. Men, mostly coloured, stand in front of shop doorways or against Morris columns;

they just stand. Older men sit in the entrances of arcades, litre bottles of wine between them. There are lines and lines of traffic, and boys running among the cars, bouncing the palms of their hands off the bonnets, and motorcyclists weaving onto the pavements. Drivers of delivery vans climb down from their vehicles, slam doors, upbraid each other.

In the faubourg itself it is nearly impossible to move. The people are four or five thick on the narrow pavements, made even narrower by the stalls of fishmongers, fruitsellers, butchers pushing outwards from the cramped shop interiors, and by the mounds of rubbish piled in the gutters between the parked cars, the crates and cardboard boxes seeping with rotting vegetables or discarded junk food, overflowing with bottles or newspapers or old bits of furniture. Old hunchbacked women and fantastically-clad negresses with babies at their hips, stand and finger apples, peppers, point to cuts of meat, debate the price of liver or brains. There is the hawking of Arabic dialect all around. A boy pushes his way out of a crowded bakery, carrying a basket with dozens and dozens of long French loaves; he calls out to make room, and it is not a boy at all, but a midget. A North African with a white beard and full robes is trying to sell an oriental carpet draped over his arm. There are five or six kebab parlours; their frying stench mingles with that of the cheese, the fish, the refuse, for it is unseasonably warm. This is where Thomas lives.

The entrance to Tommy's building is set between a fishmonger's stall and a cheese stall. Three dark little children stand in front of the doorway and look up at her; she waits for them to move: they do not. So she presses past them into the narrow passageway lit only by two naked and grimy bulbs. There is a nauseating smell in what passes for a courtyard and is dominated by two overflowing plastic bins. A rat runs off under a low wooden door, presumably of a communal lavatory. Imogen looks at the mailboxes, most of which have been broken open at some time or another, most of which carry three, four names, foreign names, crossed out or taped over as families have replaced families in these tiny apartments, or penniless students have disappeared with three months' rent unpaid, or illegal immigrants or half-crazed addicts been denounced by criminal landlords or upright neighbours. On one of these is sellotaped a slip of paper marked **HOLM Thomas.** Imogen pushes her fingers through the slot; the tips of her fingers brush the edge of an envelope. Then she starts up the perilous stairs.

On each floor are three apartments. On the first is a door bearing a Polish name, another a North African name, a third no name at all. She rings this bell and a black child, tiny, with glasses, opens the door a few inches. She has her phrase prepared – '*Je cherche le garçon anglais.*' The child gazes up at her, then puts his thumb in his mouth. Imogen shakes her head, murmurs 'Sorry', and turns away. On the second floor someone has painted his door with a life-size image of a Buckingham Palace sentry, with a spyhole exactly in the centre of his forehead. Loud pop music is playing inside. She rings the bell and a few seconds later a girl, maybe twenty-five, short and blonde and quite unremarkable-looking, opens up.

'*Je cherche le garçon anglais.*'

The girl answers in bored, heavily accented English: 'Third floor, on the right.'

On the door there is no name, no bell. It is painted white and very dirty; someone has written, in pencil,

Tommy, where are you? Of course she knocks, waits. Then she goes to the door opposite.

There is no answer. Then, as she is turning to go, she hears a woman's quavering voice: '*Qui est-ce?*' Bolts are drawn back, three or four, then a key turns in the locks. The door already has a bashed-in look. Whoever lives in this apartment must do so in constant fear. It is a woman of about sixty, bespectacled, in a dressing-gown, and not altogether clean. Imogen says in English: 'I'm looking for Thomas Holm, the English boy opposite. I'm his mother.' The woman starts to speak in rapid French, and the smell of whisky is very strong. She points to Thomas's door as she speaks, punctuating her words with high, unnerving laughs, shifting her weight from one slippered foot to the other.

'You don't speak any English?' says Imogen.

The woman laughs again, steps out unsteadily, places her emaciated hand on Imogen's arm. Her speech resembles a song, complete with little squeals, chuckles, sighs of helpless pity. But the song is devoid of meaning. It might be wry drunken humour, old woman's disapprobation, or who knows what well-founded insights into Thomas's other life: for Imogen there is only this wavering and stubby finger that points her always back to her son's impenetrable door.

Finally Imogen succeeds in extricating her arm from the garrulous woman's grip. She writes: *Thomas, please contact me ASAP at the Hotel Berlioz, Passage Jouffroy, telephone* ... – here she must dig into her bag for the hotel's brochure. She wedges the envelope into the doorframe.

Pop music is still playing in the apartment below. The blonde girl is even more impatient than before. 'No, I'm sorry, I haven't seen him. You understand, I have been for three months in Algérie. I have come back only at this weekend. Since that time I have not seen him.'

'And have you heard anything? Any noise? His flat must be directly above . . .'

'No, no,' says the girl, 'nothing at all. Usually I would hear something. There is a lot of noise, often,' she says on a note of sudden accusation.

'Well, yes, of course,' says Imogen. 'The piano —'

'It's not the piano, I don't mean that.' A man comes padding through from the back, an Arab with a moustache, wearing only underpants and obviously just out of bed. He looks at Imogen, then whispers into the girl's ear. She replies: '*Une folle. Elle cherche son fils.*' They converse briefly in French. Then the girl says in English: 'If I see him, I tell him. He knows where to look for you?' Mechanically, with the long fingernails of her right hand, she caresses the man's bare chest, watching Imogen all the time.

'And you don't know,' persists Imogen, 'who the landlady is?'

'I'm sorry, I don't understand.'

'The landlady: the owner of the flat, my son's flat.'

'Ah yes, I see. No, I don't know it. There is not a *concierge* either. I don't know, really. I am living here for one year only. Don't worry,' she says, as the man slips his arms around her neck, 'if I see him I tell him.' She turns her small face languidly up to her boyfriend, he kisses her closed eyelids. This is the limit of their assistance.

Three teenagers, two boys and a girl, are sitting at the bottom of the staircase, playing with a cigarette lighter. They look at her in alarm as she passes and huddle closer together.

She comes out into the faubourg. Once again it is inconceivable to her that Tommy should live in such a street as this. Where is the fine, airy, unpeopled Paris she expected, the smell of coffee and fresh bread, the Seine, the artists' studios, the elegant wrought-iron balconies and chaste squares? Instead there is the Faubourg Saint-Denis, blocked off and shadowed by the ghastly bulk of the triumphal archway at its end, where the pavements heave with life, where Thomas lived and was so happy for a time.

The Café de Milan is a large boulevard brasserie like any other, expensive, elegant, mediocre, with polyglot waiters unctuous and truculent by turns, and elaborate menus in multiple languages bearing long, improbable descriptions of what the dishes contain and how they are made, who created them and where and when. Imogen sits alone at a vast table, waiting for her son's friend. A waiter approaches: would Madame like an aperitif? A kir, *spécialité de la maison*? No, Madame would not.

Daniel is from Petersfield, a quarter hour by train from the Holms'. One year older than Thomas, they had been good friends at the music school and he often visited in the holidays or invited Thomas to the house of his friendly, solidly Jewish parents. In time he gave up the 'cello and turned to photography, and had the idea of going to study in a photography school in Paris. Shortly after this Thomas, too, started talking about Paris. This was the period when Imogen had not yet been won over to the exotic originality of his ambition and was still resolutely against the thought of his studying in France or indeed anywhere outside her sphere of influence, when she wildly condemned his wishes as nothing more than the desire to be different, and secretly blamed Daniel for having inspired Tommy in the first place. Tommy came to her with prospectuses, lists of famous alumni and celebrated conservatoire teachers, and in time she grew resigned, in time again wholeheartedly enthusiastic, extolling the virtues of Paris as a musical and artistic crucible and entirely given over to the innumerable merits of this city where, in fact, she had never been.

During the last vacation she asked: 'Do you still see Daniel?' 'Oh yes,' Thomas answered, 'from time to time.' Thus, when Thomas's phone rang and rang, when that disquieting postcard arrived from Susan – *He looked very different* – Imogen called Daniel's mother for his address and number in Paris.

If Daniel has always been a little bit afraid of Imogen, and he has, he is no different from the majority of Tommy's and Vicky's and Damien's and Toby's friends and many of their teachers, who have more than once experienced a sharp alarm on raising their eyes, at parents' meetings, to see among the lines of waiting parents her grand and urgent presence, impatient to flourish her list of questions about Vicky's history re-sit or Toby's violin lessons or Damien's suspected dyslexia. And the circle of those in whom she inspires a vague fear has at times extended to include her children themselves and, more particularly, her husband, principal victim of her frequent wrath, that husband who adores her and whom she detests for having rescued her from penury and given her an elegant home and financed the schooling of her daughter and sons, and who with an old man's resignation has long since concluded that he is married to a madwoman. 'Your mother's mad,' he will say with huge affection to Toby and Damien.

And if she does not keep her friends long this is more from an excess of loyalty than a lack of it, these friends being so few and she giving herself so totally, so extravagantly, that it takes only the first mistake on their part, the first letter unanswered within the arbitrary span of time mentally alotted them by Imogen, or the first vulgar or disparaging remark, she being the least vulgar of women, for her to finish with them altogether. And the excommunication comes complete with such baleful gestures of finality as packages of letters returned, Christmas invitations of long standing ostentatiously withdrawn, telephone calls cut off without a word. It is a precarious pedestal Imogen erects for those close to her, her relationships subsisting for the most part more in the operascape of her imagination than in real life, with all the inevitable disillusionments and supposed betrayals, constructing the ideal and purely imaginary friends that children create in the nursery, yet obliged to construct them from the flesh and blood of preoccupied, fallible human beings.

Daniel arrives with his girlfriend who is very blonde and very pale and who in fact turns out to be another photography student from Cologne. Both of them look young and healthy, with their casually expensive haircuts and their casually beautiful clothes, both the well-educated and well-tended children of affluent and enlightened parents, able by virtue of their privilege, their good looks, their verve to pursue a life of comfortable bohemia in the ample studios of chic colleges and at night on the terraces of cafés lately written up in deluxe youth style magazines. 'How are you?' Imogen asks. 'You look very elegant.'

They are extremely polite, studying the menu with exaggerated interest, lighting up cigarettes only after they have secured Imogen's assurances that it will not bother her in the slightest, Renata allowing herself to be interrogated as to her background, her studies, her ambitions, and answering in flawless, robotic English. A waiter hovers with a wine list, and Imogen, disconcerted because these youngsters both speak perfect French and have doubtless been brought up to know far more about wines, about seasons and vintages and methods of bottling, than she ever could, simply orders the most expensive champagne, small cause though there is for celebration.

'So,' says Daniel of the newly Americanised voice, 'I guess you want to talk about Thomas.'

She looks at him for a moment with something like her old, avaricious, artistic curiosity, looks at his beautiful strong Jewish face, the wonderful teeth and excellent bones, and thinks she could perhaps sculpt a real David out of him, a real earthy warrior of Zion to repudiate the Greeked-up, camply muscular David peddled by Michelangelo.

'I'm afraid I can't tell you very much. You know, Thomas came to Paris nearly two years ago. He called me up a couple of times, we met for a coffee, that sort of thing. He didn't know anybody here. Then he started at the Conservatoire and I guess he must have found some people there. I was very busy; we didn't see so much of each other. He was living in a little room in the Marais, then he got another place, miles from anywhere. I guess you must know all this already.

'I thought he'd changed very much since school, he'd got a lot more confident. He gave a party once, this was when he was already living in the apartment at Strasbourg Saint-Denis. I guess he wouldn't even have invited me except that by chance we met that day at the market, and he said he was giving this party, did I want to come? There were maybe thirty people, all of them crowded into his tiny apartment. I didn't know anybody. He introduced me to his girlfriend Véronique.

She's a film student. Well, I talked to her for quite a while, she was just about the only person I talked to all night. She said she had been going out with Tommy about six months. That was back in June.

'I was surprised at the number of people he knew. I would say maybe half the people there were French, half foreigners. You know how when he came to Paris he could hardly speak a word of French. Well, by the time he gave this party he was pretty fluent, I guess thanks to this girlfriend of his. Véronique, she has an American mother and she speaks English like an American, but I know they only ever spoke French together. And there were people there – I mean, my God, you can't imagine. Americans, Australians, Yugoslavs, Italians. It was a regular United Nations joint. I said to him, "Tommy, where'd you pick them all up?" He just laughed. I guess a lot of them were musicians from the Conservatoire – it's always a pretty mixed bunch there. But actually not so many. There were students and actors and models too, and others who were, well, I couldn't even begin to guess. And then of course there were friends of this Véronique.'

Imogen, alert to the distant, newly transatlantic inflections of the earnest little boy who eight years ago stood by her kitchen table as she made a cake and then solemnly requested the recipe for his mother, folds her hands on the table. 'Véronique,' she says: 'tell me about her.' Then, suddenly conscious that they are excluding the German girl from the conversation, she asks: 'Do *you* know Thomas?'

A look passes between Renata and Daniel. 'No,' says Renata, 'I don't.'

Daniel empties his glass of champagne. He has ordered some fish dish, very elegantly presented, very insubstantial. 'What is there to tell? I only saw her a few times, at this party of Tommy's and then at another party she gave in her own apartment a few weeks later. She's very pretty, very French, although like I say she's half-American. I don't know how she took up with Tommy or where they met. She broke up with Tommy a few months later, that's all I know. At her party she was very busy, naturally, with all her friends, but at one point she came up and asked me if I wanted to talk, and we went down into the street for half an hour or so. Thomas, in any case, had taken over the guests. She said Tommy wanted her to let him move in with her, into her flat. She has a big apartment – well, big by Paris standards, two rooms – and she couldn't afford it on her own; she had to find somebody to share it with her, but she wasn't sure about that somebody being Tommy. She asked me what I thought about it . . . well, what could I say? Tommy was a friend of mine. I asked her what the problem was, and she said she didn't actually see the relationship lasting so much longer. This was end of June. And as it happened, of course, she was right, they broke up sometime later that summer. Tommy went off to Spain, and apparently —'

'To *Spain*?' exclaims Imogen.

Renata is smiling faintly to herself. Daniel looks across at Imogen. 'Yes, to Spain. He didn't tell you?' There is a brief hiatus as the waiter approaches to take their orders for dessert. Then Imogen asks, lowering her voice as if this same waiter might hear, understand, and care: 'Last summer? This was last summer?'

'Yes, in July.'

'But, in July he was at a summer school in Nice. Two weeks.'

'No,' says Daniel, 'I guess he didn't go. He went to Spain. You know, we'd talked vaguely about travelling back to England together for the summer vacation. He was going to the summer course in Nice. Then he called me up, said he'd changed his plans, that he was going to Spain with a boy called Thierry. This boy was at Véronique's party too. Tommy always seemed to be going somewhere or other. Well. He said that he was going to Spain, so he'd be travelling back to England later than planned.' He pauses. 'You didn't know this? But surely —'

At the end of last July Imogen had received a postcard from Nice, the Promenade des Anglais: 'Having fun, working hard, three hours of classes a day, will ring you.' She received a phone call from Nice, from a payphone: 'I've only got a few francs, I can't talk, just to say I'll be back on the second. You don't have to meet me, I'll make my own way . . .' The phone shut off, and on the second of August Tommy arrived back with a modest suntan and various amusing stories about the summer music course.

'Well,' says Daniel, lighting a cigarette. 'At this party Thomas talked to me about the Conservatoire, how it was beginning to bore him. He told me he'd made a lot of other friends in the music world, very important people, but at the same time he was very secretive about it, wouldn't tell me who these people were – even though the names would probably not have meant anything to me. He seemed very excited about something or other – you know, torn between the desire to make an impression and the need to keep it a secret. He would give just so much away and then shut up completely. Of course, I believed what he was telling me; even so, I remember wondering where this Thierry, for example, fitted into his new circle of friends.

'Thierry: you might try finding him. He's an actor, which actually means that he's out of work most of the time. When I met him he was working in a bar in the Marais. He saw a lot of Tommy, I know that. I'll give you the address of the bar.' Renata places her hand on his wrist and whispers in his ear, but he brushes her off irritably. He takes out a gold-plated ballpoint and a small white business card with *Daniel Solomon, photographe* printed on it, and scribbles on the back. As he does so he glances up at Imogen. 'Are you worried?'

'Of course I'm worried,' she says. 'Wouldn't you be?' She turns her empty glass round and round on the tablecloth. The waiter arrives with dessert and she looks at it vacantly. She has eaten approximately a quarter of what has been set before her. She says: 'Daniel. Do you think he may be in some kind of trouble?'

'Let's hope not, shall we,' says Daniel.

Immaculate, flawlessly polite Daniel. 'Well, if I can be of any further help in any way, please don't hesitate to call me.'

The young people are preparing to leave. Daniel has given her the address of Thierry's bar, and also explained, to the best of his ability, how to find where Véronique lives, or at least lived ten months ago. 'I never knew her second name,' he says, 'and I never had a telephone number for her. I was at her place just this once, and someone else took me, but I remember it quite well; it looked out onto Sacré-Coeur.' This over, Imogen heroically steers the conversation back onto neutral ground – heroically, given that her only thought now is to leave this smart, polite young couple to their light, comfortable apartment and their elegant, international friends, their brunches on the terraces of American diners and their cheques from home, their fashion shows in elegant hotels and their parties given in discothèques by promising young film directors, while Tommy, her son, wanders lost somewhere in a Paris of cancelled addresses, unanswered messages, disturbing associations.

So they chatter inconsequentially over coffee, even laughing a little at reminiscences of Daniel's boyhood visits to the house in Haslemere and of her own visits to the music school: 'All the teachers were terrified of you, you know,' he says. 'You appeared at the staff-room door as if you were ready for battle.' She forbears to ask if Tommy has ever spoken about her over the years: she is intelligent enough to have no illusions that he would do so charitably, and intelligent enough not much to care, believing this to be the lot of mothers who devote themselves to their children, and content to be a rock of everlasting in the flux of his young life, a point to be returned to in times of need, moments independent of affection and of intimacy, both of which she abjured in an early self-sacrifice which, did she but know it, was born of her own devouring maternal need.

Even so, she asks Daniel if he would take her to Thierry's bar sometime. His face shutters: he is so sorry, he is so busy . . . Renata, standing there willowy and blonde, thanks her, thanks her very much for the dinner. The three of them leave the restaurant and walk along the boulevard as far as the taxi stand.

'Where might you find him? I wish I could tell you. You see, we went our own separate ways very much, here in Paris. Perhaps it was my fault. I guess I wasn't so helpful to him in the beginning as I might have been. Then later, as I said, he had all these other friends, a whole new circle. I wasn't part of Thomas's circle.'

He folds himself comfortably behind Renata into a taxi. Already, as she smiles and waves back, Imogen is fingering Daniel's card in her coat pocket. She walks along to the next taxi, whose driver speaks a little English. Sinking back into the seat she directs him towards the Marais.

The bar is small and very crowded. One wall is dominated by a huge mirrored 1950s-style clockface, and a 1950s jukebox stands elaborately and redundantly in the corner. The barmen are young and muscular. Behind the bar, among an assortment of bottles, is a stand with magazines whose cover displays a nude man of twenty or so. The customers are for the most part between eighteen and thirty years old. They are slim, smooth-faced, preternaturally clean, and the dress is predominantly leather or denim. Some wear small pieces of jewellery, while others are clad to excess with dress shirts and silk scarves and little caps on hair variously bleached, dyed, hennaed, and freakishly styled. There are two or three girls in the bar, very white-faced, very made-up, with punkish clothes and a lot of junk jewellery. They giggle together, annexed to a group of theatrical, strident men. There are other groups around the tables. There are the men who sit in couples, without speaking. Then there are the single men sitting at the bar or leaning against the wall, and these look at each other from time to time, then look at their newspapers or at their exquisite hands or at their glasses of beer. There are mirrors on the walls and behind the bar, and sometimes the men look at each other in these mirrors, sometimes they stare and stare.

There is very loud disco music playing. A waiter, small, smiling, immaculate, trips in and out between the tables, exchanging remarks here and there, touching the arm of somebody, tousling the hair of somebody else.

Three people get up to leave. As they push their way to the door they call to another group, and there is an exchange of laughter. Everything appears very friendly. Imogen shuffles in behind the table vacated.

The waiter begins to clear the table without, it appears, noticing her at all. He is just lifting the ashtray when he glances at her with excessive surprise and flings out a question in French.

'Do you speak English?' she asks.

He strikes a pose. 'Of coeursse. What would you laaqque?'

Imogen looks round at the other tables. Most people are drinking beer. 'A beer, please.'

'*Trente-trois*, Kronenbourg, Pelforth?'

Imogen gestures her incomprehension. The waiter smiles with some parts of his face and disappears.

She looks up. A boy at the next table is watching her. When she looks at him he does not look away but turns up his smile as if it were an instrument of illumination to be manipulated at will. He is about twenty, with very dark and long-lashed eyes in a tanned face, thick black hair. He wears a black shirt with a yellow sleeveless pullover and trousers of some pale uncrushable fabric. There is an empty coffee cup in front of him, a packet of cigarettes, a folded newspaper.

The waiter is back with her beer. 'Twelve francs, please,' he says to the square of wall behind her head. She gives him fifteen.

'Excuse me,' she says, and he turns back to her, his eyes wide. 'Excuse me, but do you know where I can find Thierry? I think he works here.'

He tilts his head from one side to the other. 'Thierry has not worked here since maybe six months,' he says. At a nearby table people are looking at them in frank amusement. Evidently this waiter is a valued and pet jester of the neighbourhood. She presses on: 'But do you know where he is now?'

'I don't know. Maybe I can ask.' He moves off to another table. The boy with dark hair is still watching her.

Twenty minutes later she has finished her beer and the waiter is nowhere to be seen. Another group has moved in, older men with moustaches. Imogen picks up her coat and makes for the bar; the little waiter has disappeared and his two tough, muscular colleagues lean over the counter and chat with the new arrivals. She stands for a moment, jostled by customers pressing their way to the back of the room, then steps out into the street. Two young men stand on the pavement, looking at the ground, not exchanging a word. There are no taxis here and she reaches into her bag for the map of Paris, when there at her side is the dark boy with his dazzling smile. He touches her elbow.

'Pierre Saporito,' he says. 'I used to know Thierry. Maybe I can find out for you where he is.' With great ease he slips a square of paper into her open handbag. 'That,' he says, 'is my telephone number. Now you can call me whenever you wish.'

She reaches out a hand after him, calls out: 'Wait.' But he has already disappeared down a yellow-lit sidestreet. She turns to the two young men, who continue just to stare at the ground, oblivious to her presence there.

Musical statues

Given that she arrived in Paris only a few hours ago, she has not done too badly. She has heard about the existence of this girlfriend, she for whom Tommy has never had a girlfriend. In fact she has always ascribed this fact to his absorption in his studies which leaves him so little time and energy for relationships; she has preferred not to dwell on it, telling herself always and only that he will 'sort himself out in time', without even noticing the implicit admission that something is amiss. She has seen the place where Thomas lives and which he described to her on a postcard over a year ago, the day he found it, 'in a run-down and picturesque end of town, full of street markets, wonderful old courtyards and characters and crazy neighbours'. She has heard of parties he gave, friends he invited, he who never cared for parties, who had a small circle of schoolfriends devoted to him and to whom he scarcely wrote, scarcely phoned in the holidays, preferring to stay indoors all day and read or watch television or practise the piano, exquisitely polite when there was company at the house but always retiring early to bed, aloof from his stepbrothers' pals and his sister's boyfriends as he was from his own friends and family. She has heard for the first time that the Conservatoire 'bored' him, after all his efforts to win her over to the idea, after all their difficulties in procuring him a place, after all the glowing reports given out during Sunday telephone calls and vacations when asked if Paris life suited him, if French teaching was really so much better than English, if he did not regret his decision, etc. She has learned of a holiday in Spain undertaken when Tommy was to her knowledge attending an annual summer school in Nice, sending postcards, calling home, laughing about the teachers, complaining about the food. She has visited a bar which, if Tommy himself never frequented, is a gathering-place for certain among that shadowy group unambiguously described by Daniel as 'Thomas's circle'.

So she is nearer to finding Thomas than she knows. But it is not in her nature to be content. So, for her, it appears that Tommy can have been frolicking in Spain when she thought him working in France, can have contemplated moving in with a girlfriend when she believed him to be sexless or worse, have been mingling with strange company in dark and curious rooms when she placed him on some bright and cheery terrace drinking coffee and exchanging jokes with earnest music students. The question of Tommy's honesty is relatively unimportant: what matters is that the hints and warnings of this evening have once more raised for her the spectre conjured by Susan's postcard and by its tormenting picture of Tommy – standing on that pavement, climbing into that car – as being irrecoverable. For it is her quest to recover Tommy, as all heroines have a quest, and she would be the less heroic were she so soon to recognise that finding something means discovery as well as recovery; that – as with Eurydice – it is rarely intact that the hero brings back his treasure from the darkness where it was lost; and that in bringing it to light this treasure can be lost more thoroughly than if he had never braved the shadows to go down after it.

But Tommy is in danger, Daniel has all but said so, and this thought alone must occupy her, not the audacity with which he planned and executed a jaunt in Spain while giving his mother to believe he was working hard in Nice; nor the airy guiltlessness with which he sought to amuse himself in a Paris paid for materially out of the depleted funds of his mother's marriage and emotionally out of the long years of her unswerving and sleepless devotion. Nor is there for her any real distinction between the material question and the emotional, for the financial comfort which permitted Thomas's Parisian adventure was dearly bought, her wealthy second marriage having been contracted and maintained in a definite spirit of self-sacrifice.

But she cannot start blaming Tommy now. And so, on reaching her hotel, although it is long past midnight, she calls up her husband in Haslemere, informs him that she will be absent for several more days, that he will have to manage as best he can, that she has not yet found Tommy but is sure of doing so. It is for the sheer reassuring normality of being irritated by him, of being able to spend her vexation, that she telephones, scornfully berating the old-man's helplessness in his voice. For she is dangerously convinced that, whatever her mistakes, her chosen course of action has always been the only right one, and so she feels no moral compunction about rounding on her husband in private or in public while all the time spending his money on the exclusive education of her children by a previous marriage.

Her room looks drab in the weak yellow light. The window is stiff and when she pulls at it some white paint flakes off on her fingers. She sits for a while listening to the night traffic away in the rue du Faubourg Montmartre. The day Thomas arrived in Paris he had no address to go to, knew no one apart from Daniel, who was in any case away on holiday somewhere. He deposited his suitcase at the Gare Saint-Lazare and walked the city with his shoulder-bag, and, after enquiring about fifty times in his limited schoolboy French, found a cheap hotel up near Pigalle. To his naive and untravelled eyes there seemed to be nothing special about this place beyond an astonishing amount of dirt. In fact it was an *hotel de passe*, few of its rooms taken for more than an hour. That evening, after wandering along the Seine and buying himself a cheap dinner in a boisterous family restaurant in the Quartier Latin, he sat thus in front of his window and watched the paved street below, where the whores, pimps and customers passed and repassed, approached, withdrew, returned, joined, departed, returned, separated, their movements seemingly as choreographed as in some classical ballet and astonishingly beautiful. Thomas, who had never in his life seen a whore to know she was a whore, felt a breathless exultation at being in Paris and at the prospect of living in Paris for years to come. He was nineteen years old. Months later, back in England for Christmas, he attempted to describe that first evening, but could not convey all he had felt of its poetry.

Imogen seldom listened to his stories anyway, or did so distractedly. But what about the Conservatoire, how many hours do you practise a day, who have you met, what's the competition like, are you working, working, working? So on the rare occasions when Thomas tried to tell her stories about Paris she would hear them with mounting irritation: *that's* not what you went there for. She could probably have learned many things from him about Paris, but instead the city has remained for her something mythical, a romantic folly consisting not of air and walls and people but of some fantastic idea immaterially built on the pages of expatriate writers of the 1920s and on the canvases of her beloved Impressionists. Even now she does not see Paris, carnivalesque, occurring all around her. She notices that the city is dirty, its inhabitants trenchant, its prices exaggerated. The thought goes through her head that Paris can no longer be what once it was, without her realising that the same could be said of all the cities of Europe, whose golden ages were never more than the accumulated phrases and assembled colours of purely accidental configurations of certain talented writers and certain gifted painters who themselves wrote and painted from the fugitive memories of what they had seen. For the poetry of a city exists in its very passing, and no one ever lives in a golden age but only reads of it years later, or, turning a corner in a gallery, discovers it on a canvas already centuries old. No light existed such as a painter rendered it, no woman was ever so beautiful, nor any café breathed an atmosphere so conducive to bright or subtle conversation as was not, days or years later, in groaning solitude, polished and adorned by the artist who fondly remembered it. No one lives in a golden age unless all ages are golden, golden not with the bright metallic gleam of imperial splendour but with the autumnal glow of leaves turned so rich a colour only by virtue of their past, recollected, eternally vanishing green.

The expensive, petroleum-scented terrace of the Café de la Paix. She takes a postcard and writes, mechanically: 'The city is very beautiful . . .' Would she, in other circumstances, appreciate, even enjoy, this her first visit to Paris? She has no curiosity whatsoever about foreign countries or in fact about anywhere on earth beyond her houses in Haslemere and London and Wales and the schools and colleges where her children are educated. And indeed since the age of thirty, that watershed year in which she made her second marriage, she has never embarked on a journey in any other spirit than that of desperate need or urgent duty.

She finishes her second 'breakfast' of black coffee and pays. There are lines of taxis in front of the opera house and she takes one, giving Véronique's address. Daniel does not know Véronique's surname. Martin, she reads on the mailboxes downstairs, Charpenet, Pascal & Annick Doucet – then there is a square of yellow paper with little drawings of birds and hearts on it, and the calligraphed words: *Véronique La Besque et Stéphanie Duporge, 2ème étage à gauche.* Imogen hauls out her pocket French-English dictionary – *gauche* means left, among other things. The staircase is carpeted and fairly clean, in sharp contrast to Tommy's building.

A blonde girl of about twenty answers. Imogen has prepared no explanation, has not thought beyond this moment, she stands there as if her remarkable presence alone were sufficient explanation. After a few seconds it becomes obvious that this is not so. 'Véronique?'

'*Elle n'est pas là*,' says the girl.

'Do you speak English? *Parlez-vous . . . ?*' The girl nods, bored, does not relinquish hold of the door. 'I'm looking for Véronique. Does she live here?'

'She is not here. She is at the school. I can give a message to her?'

'When will she be back?'

'Perhaps three, perhaps four, perhaps five. Who shall I tell is looking for her?'

'My name is Imogen Holm. I'm Thomas's mother.' The girl makes an irritated gesture of incomprehension. Imogen repeats: 'Thomas Holm. He is a friend of Véronique's. I'm his mother.'

The girl stares at her, then, amused, nods three or four times. 'I see. Well. Thomas, *ça alors*.' She gives an insolent little laugh. '*Mon Dieu, Thomas*.' She pronounces it as if it were a French name: 'Tomah'.

Imogen's mouth tightens at the girl's demeanour. 'You know him?'

The girl shrugs her shoulders, looks Imogen up and down. Then: 'No. No, I don't know Thomas. Véronique . . . *eh bien*. So you wish to speak with Véronique?'

'Yes, I do, if you could let me know when she'll be here, please? If I come back at four o'clock, will that be all right? It's very important.'

'Important,' says the girl, smiling at the floor. '*Mon Dieu*, well yes, perhaps she will be back, perhaps not. She finishes at the school at three, perhaps she will come straight home, perhaps not.'

Imogen opens her mouth to ask another question, closes it again, then says: 'I will come back, then, at four o'clock.' And now she must occupy herself for six hours with only the rankling memory of this awful girl who seems to know all about Tommy without ever having met him, because she shares Véronique's apartment and knows her well and because after all Véronique stepped out of Thomas's life ten months ago and has since moved on, just as the boy who worked in the bar has moved on, in the weird inevitable flux of Paris. Why should she expect these people to be as they were when Thomas found them, why imagine that time stopped at that moment and that now they are transfixed and frozen as in some game of musical statues, and only awaiting a sign from her to release them from their immobility.

Six hours. Rue Steinkerque is full of women examining and selecting lengths of cloth at huge cut-price fabric emporia, tourists queueing for ice-creams or postcards before venturing up the hill. An old man with a green plastic marmoset on his shoulder plays a hurdy-gurdy. On the steps leading up to Sacré-Coeur very black men in fantastically garlanded robes and hats lay out rugs of African jewellery or manipulate chirping painted wooden birds, or unsmilingly reach out to visitors, arms looped round many times with long strands of beads. In front of the church a woman approaches Imogen and presses her to buy a religious image. She looks up at Sacré-Coeur, no longer white as it appeared from a distance, and debates whether or not to join the terrifying numbers of people who strain towards the entrance. A man of about forty wearing a pale grey suit grins up at her widely and lifts his polaroid camera; involuntarily and awkwardly she smiles. He strides up to her with the result which, he informs her in his fluid hard-sell French-English, will cost her only twenty francs. 'Only twenty francs! For picture of beautiful you in front beautiful Sacré-Coeur! Is a gift, *non*?' She buys the picture, at which another vendor of Catholic artefacts makes towards her.

She wanders the streets of Montmartre that she scarcely noticed before. In a café she waits for a quarter of an hour to be served by the huge *patronne* herself. Coffee lukewarm, sandwich stale. In the Place des Abbesses she distractedly admires the Guimaud metro entrance, until some leather-clad men begin to rev up their bicycles right behind her and she moves on, arriving at the Place du Tertre where at last she has the gratification of regarding with contempt the execrable sketches of the professional artists, and can allow herself a world-weary sigh at the fall from grace of this once-village home of her favourite Impressionist painters. It is only twenty-five past twelve. She buys an English-language Paris guide in a newsagent. Reaching for her purse she finds the photograph of herself which she bought an hour before for twenty francs, and looks at it for the first time: a tall woman in the disdained beauty of her middle age, her gaunt unloved face caught smiling lopsidedly at a stranger in a foreign city. She stares at it. The shop-girl clears her throat impatiently. Imogen hands over a two hundred franc note and the girl slams her change down on the counter.

She visits the Gustave Moreau Museum near Pigalle but is soon irritated by the obsessive canvases with their tawdry depictions of purgatorial or Babylonic scenes. Once more out in the sunlight she rubs her eyes. She is in Paris, where should she go? Where goes every visitor to Paris the unforgettable? She hails a taxi and asks to be taken to the Quartier Latin. The driver smiles to himself: as if the Quartier Latin were a huddle of actual streets, a geographic reality and not a myth fostered by generations of the rapacious guardians of the city's eternal prosperity and invincible self-regard. He drives her to the Place Saint-Michel.

She tries to find a payphone to call Tommy again, but all are either vandalised or equipped only for phone-cards. She sits down on the terrace of one of the plush riverside cafés and orders a Perrier from a waiter in a long white smock. Americans, blond and tanned, Germans, tanned and blond, talk and laugh all around her. She drinks her Perrier, goes down to the cloakroom and uses the phone, but Thomas is not there. Then she calls Daniel. 'He's not at home, I'm afraid,' says Renata. 'He will be back this evening. Have you been successful in finding your son?'

'Not yet,' says Imogen. 'When will Daniel be back?'

'This evening as I say. At about eight o'clock. But then we will go to a cinema. I shall tell him you have called.'

The Boulevard Saint-Michel, much celebrated in verse and song, is lined now with boutiques, shoe shops, cinemas, pizza and hamburger joints, characterless bookstores. Young people sit around the fountain nursing cans of beer and picking at portions of chips. The boulevard gets more boring the further she goes, and she turns back for the river and the quayside booksellers' stalls. She buys a beautiful expensive book of black and white photographs for Tommy; then, feeling guilty because he is her favourite, goes back to the stall and buys a book of Monet reproductions for Vicky. In the centre of the river are the two serene and silver islands from out of which the city of Paris medievally spread. She walks along the leafy quayside as far as the Tour d'Argent. Here it is almost peaceful. She sits on a low stone wall with her back to the river. She knows that what she can see about her in every direction is beautiful: thousands have said it. But all this beauty leaves her quite cold, and it is not the mere fact of Tommy's disappearance and her consequent preoccupation which leaves her so frigid to Paris's seductions. She, more than anyone, values beauty: has not her life been one long struggle to wrest some beauty from the intractable matter of paint and canvas, have her eyes not sought this alone, her arms not worked and worked at it? But she is greedy for beauty, with a real and physical greed. Perhaps this is why she returns again and again to painting the land around her house in Haslemere or the wooded hill behind her house in Wales or the faces and forms of models she can choose and hire by the hour; perhaps why in a sense she cares as much for the music-making of her children as for her own art; perhaps why the reproductions in the art books she compulsively buys mean more to her, at this moment, than the sunlight on the porous stones of Paris, since these books can at least give her an illusion of possession. And this greed is nowhere more evident than in her houses themselves, each of which she has made a consummate expression of her contradictory spirit, where each painting, each item of furniture lends a separate and unique vitality to the wall where it hangs, the corner it occupies, and where for years she has arranged parties and dinners not with a hostess's spontaneous largesse but with a maniacal painter's eye for detail. And in the centre of the canvas are placed her children, so undifferentiated from her artworks as to be nearly fleshless and fatherless, offspring of some immaculate conception, as if divinely willed to birth for no other purpose than to make whole the picture.

She wanders back along the quays, past the bulky rear of Notre Dame, past Shakespeare and Company, that famous American bookstore run by an ageing and eccentric expatriate, where Thomas in his first naive months of wonderment in Paris spent his evenings, sometimes helping out at the cashdesk or stacking books in the dusty, dim recesses of the shop, chatting with other young and impoverished travellers and with the continental poets and drifters in their twenties and thirties, the students of art and the aspiring photographers and cineastes, crashing out on each other's floors in the tiny garret rooms they had managed to sublet for three months or six months in the Quartier Latin or in Montmartre, and who were looking for jobs as language teachers or as *au pairs* or as office boys in international companies or waiters in American restaurants, and who in the meantime attended crash courses in French at the Sorbonne and each day came in their artistic idleness to hang around this store and discuss the astronomical rents of apartments or the impossibility of acquiring a residency permit. And the same cast of wanly hopeful exiles and orphans, when the shop closed at midnight, could be found seated around a couple of tables in one of the huge cafés along the Boulevard Saint-Michel, sneered at by beautiful and immaculate waiters, ordering the cheapest jug of prudently unidentified house wine, then, at two, as the staff started mopping the floor under their feet and stacking the chairs on the tables around them, over to the rue Saint-Jacques and a colourless bar for local alcoholics, jean-clad teenage couples and lone wolves posing over the pinball machine, pooling their francs for one more round of drinks, feeding the jukebox and dancing between the tables in absurd couplings, until the jovial barman drove them out at four; when it was on down to Polly Maggoo, grabbing a hamburger or strip of pizza on the way, shuffling through the bar to a free table amidst the hardened drugtakers and cool, sharply-dressed thugs, waiting with eager dread for a fight to break out or the police to raid, fingering their passports in handbags or inner pockets, wondering about the going rate for marijuana but too nervous to ask, talking and talking until the dawn and the metro and their tiny, exorbitant skylit rooms perched over six flights of stairs, the expatriate youth of the city, tomorrow to recollect and recommence in Shakespeare and Company, legendary institution where Imogen will never go, where she will never even know that Thomas passed his first glorious weeks, had his first intoxicating successes, in Paris.

'I'm sorry, Véronique is not yet here.'

But this time Imogen is ready. 'Fine, I'll wait.'

The girl widens her eyes. 'Of course. Of course. Come in.' Some Vivaldi music sounds faintly from a cassette deck somewhere in the flat. The girl holds out a hand for Imogen's coat. 'Please come through.'

They are in a high, white airy room; only one corner of the ceiling is browned with damp. Sacré-Coeur, through a window, appears somehow more impressive than usual. The girl gestures her in the direction of the sofa-bed. The room is pleasantly untidy. 'Would you like a coffee?'

'No thank you,' says Imogen. 'Who are you, please?'

The girl is astonished. 'Stéphanie. Stéphanie Duporge. I share this apartment with Véronique.' She seems rather subdued by Imogen now, stands watching her visitor as if waiting for instructions.

'Please don't let me disturb you. I'll just sit here and wait.'

The girl picks up a packet of cigarettes, waves them towards Imogen, lights one for herself. 'Excuse me, this apartment is so untidy.' Then she says: 'It's about Thomas?'

'Yes.'

'Yes.' She moves about the room, swaying her compact young body. 'You are sure you don't want to drink something?' Imogen shakes her head. 'We have some orange juice here. Or wine.' The Vivaldi concerto comes to an end. 'Have you seen him? Thomas?'

'Not yet,' says Imogen. After a moment Stéphanie says 'Excuse me' and disappears into the next room. A few seconds later Imogen hears her talking softly into the telephone.

She sits, waits, stands up, walks around the room. There is a large framed montage of photographs over the desk, some of them very professional, including some shots of Manhattan skyscrapers from seemingly impossible angles, and others of a Venice that gives the impression of melting into its own waters. But there are several people shots as well. Stéphanie appears in some of them: at a table in an outdoor Mediterranean restaurant, on the riverbank of a German or Scandinavian city, costumed and made up as a witch for a party. And there are several of another girl, smallish, pretty, serious, with straight dark-red hair. There are no pictures of Thomas.

The door opens and the red-haired girl comes into the room, already tugging at her jacket. On seeing Imogen she stops. 'Véronique,' says Imogen.

The girl begins to say something in French. At that moment Stéphanie appears in the other doorway and addresses her friend rapidly, quietly. Then she shrugs, takes one last look at them both, and goes back into her room. Slowly, now, as if on display, Véronique removes her jacket, drapes it carefully over the back of a chair. She apologises for having kept her visitor waiting as if they had some kind of appointment. Then she says: I'm sorry, I really need a coffee. Can I get you one?'

She goes off to the kitchen. There is no trace of an accent, she sounds quite American, she looks like a girl who works hard and has few friends. She looks, also, kind. Why should she not be kind?

After a few moments Véronique returns with the coffee. 'Well, now,' she says.

'Well.' And Imogen explains why she is in Paris, explains about Thomas's silence, about the postcard from Susan, about her conversation with Daniel – 'Ah yes,' says Véronique, 'the Jewish boy' – and how she came to find this apartment.

Véronique waits for her to finish, then sits, rubbing her wrists together. 'And now I guess you want to know where Thomas is.'

'Do you know?'

'I'm sorry. I saw Thomas two months ago. We met in a discothèque. He was with a whole bunch of people, I was with a whole bunch of others. He didn't introduce me to his friends, I didn't introduce him to mine. We talked for ten minutes, maybe. He didn't say he had any plans to go anywhere but' – smile – 'why should he tell me anything? He said . . . what? That he was still in the same apartment, at Strasbourg Saint-Denis. He had no plans to move, so far as I could tell. He said the piano was going really well, he had the best teacher in France. He said. I asked him about his plans, he told me he was staying in Paris for another two years at least. He asked if I wanted to go over and see him sometime. I said that, really, no, I didn't much. Then we said goodbye.'

'That was all?'

'As you say, that was all.'

'When was this?'

'About two months ago. Beginning of March, I guess.'

'And how did he seem to you?'

'I don't understand.'

'Did he seem well? His health? Did he seem . . . all right?'

Véronique considers for a moment. 'Yes, he was very well. As always. He was always well. I never saw him when he wasn't well, I never saw him when he looked tired; it's what I most remember about him. He always looked like an advertisement for some vitamin drink or something. He never got ill, he never got tired out —'

'Unhappy, then. Did he seem unhappy?'

'Thomas?' The girl lets out a snort of laughter. 'Thomas unhappy?' Then she is serious again. 'No, no, he wasn't unhappy at all. At least, if he was, he certainly didn't let on to me. But then — ' She drains her coffee straightaway. 'Are you worried?'

'Of course. Wouldn't you be?'

Véronique considers the question a moment, lets it pass. Then, deliberately provocative: 'How much do you know about me?'

'Nothing. What I told you. What Daniel told me.'

'Thomas never told you about me?' She waits; when there is no answer she smiles to herself. 'Did you know about his holiday in Spain?'

Imogen does not reply. It only increases her jealousy of the girl that she should know about it too.

'You know,' Véronique continues, 'it was the most awful thing I ever did, sending that postcard to you. I don't know why I did it, I don't know how I could have done it. He came over the evening before he was due to leave. I wasn't expecting him, we were already seeing each other less and less, it was obvious that the whole relationship was already over. He said to me: "So, you're going down south for the summer, is that it?" I don't know how he knew, I didn't tell him. I have some family down there. He gave me the postcard and said would I post it sometime, maybe a week later? I asked him why he'd written it. It was a postcard of Nice, you know, you must remember. He just said that you'd paid a lot of money for this summer course in Nice, that he didn't want to go but that he didn't want you to be hurt either. That was how he got me to do it, by telling me how hurt you'd be if you knew.

'Well, I took the postcard. I guess I should have thrown it out with the garbage right away but, hell, when I got down to Aix, sure enough I still had it. I sent it. When I came back to Paris a month later there was a postcard from Spain, from Thomas, saying how we were through but how he still wanted us to be friends. I wasn't angry. We'd been past tense for some time.'

She is lighting a cigarette as she says this, and at this precise moment the telephone rings and she breaks off, still holding aloft the smoking match. Stéphanie appears in the doorway – '*J'arrive*,' says Véronique. But first she pulls open a drawer in the desk, rummages around, and brings out a large brown envelope which she tosses over to Imogen. 'Here, take a look at these. Maybe you'll find them interesting.'

There is not much in the envelope. The postcard from the carnival in Barcelona. Scrupulously Imogen checks the postmark: July 28th of the previous year – with its message half in French, half in English:

> Qu'ils sont séduisants, ces Espagnols! Maybe I'll stay here forever, lying in the sun under the huge sky. In any case I've been able to do a lot of thinking here,

and as you've probably guessed, decided it's time to call a halt. Ne me pleure pas, ma belle, it's for the best. Je serai toujours ton meilleur ami, n'est-ce pas?

Mille tendresses.

Thomas.

Another card, not sent through the post, a nineteenth century daguerreotype picture of a huddle of narrow streets and alleyways in a poor quarter of Paris; on the back is Thomas's name and a date. Then there is a photograph of Tommy at a party standing with another boy and talking to a third, whose arm and hand alone appear in the frame. Now, contemplating the picture of Thomas with his hair over his eyes, with a glass and a cigarette in one hand and gesturing with the other, she is struck by his resemblance to Daniel, and to that other boy from last night's bar, a resemblance which is not at all superficial, since physically they are very different, but which stems from the confidence, the easy grace of the very handsome and the very young. She thinks: men were not so beautiful in my day. She remembers Tommy, awkward, coltish, at sixteen. Where has he acquired this confidence, how is it that he is able to shoulder his way through this hectic other life calm, intact, effortless?

Véronique returns from her telephone conversation. Imogen holds up the postcard and asks: 'Did he always sign himself Thomas?'

'Oh sure. He insisted on it. He couldn't bear the name Tommy, he said. Some people called him that, in the beginning, but he didn't like it at all.'

Imogen says: 'You know, on his door, the door to his flat, here, in Paris, someone had written "Tommy, where are you?"'

'Really. Ah well,' says Véronique, plainly not much

interested. 'Maybe he changed his mind. Or maybe it was someone who didn't know him so well.' She goes over to the chair and picks up her jacket. 'Listen, I'm very sorry, but I just had a telephone call and I have to leave in half an hour. I really am sorry. Maybe there's something more I can do – if I think of anything, sure, I'll let you know. But really I doubt . . .'

'Please,' says Imogen, folding her hands together and staring hard at them, 'please: are you sure you have no idea where he might be? I can see that perhaps now you're not friends, but surely you wouldn't want . . . surely you understand? Or where I can go . . . don't you know any friends of his, anyone special?'

'Have you tried the Conservatoire?' asks Véronique, suddenly quite practical, disinterested. 'That seems to me the most obvious place to start. Surely he'd tell them if he was planning to go away somewhere. As to friends –' here she laughs '– ah, well, you'll have your work cut out finding those.'

'What do you mean? He has so many friends.'

'Yes, but remember. I knew him only a year ago. I doubt if any of the friends he had then lasted the course. None of us lasted very long. In a sense I probably had the record.'

Imogen asks: 'Why do you hate him so much?'

Véronique shrugs her shoulders, as if tired of the whole proceeding. It is unsettling to see these little Gallic betrayals, all the while hearing the girl's mellifluously American voice. 'Hate? You don't understand. *Enfin.*' She sits down again, exhales cigarette smoke, looks squarely at Imogen. 'Sometime early on – we'd been going out . . . maybe two months? No more. He persuaded me to go to the Faubourg Saint-Honoré and buy a dress costing seven thousand francs. Which was about all the money I had at the time for the whole semester. The idea was that we wanted to go to some really smart nightclub and he said I had to dress right. I'm sure he didn't particularly like the dress. I'm sure we would have got into the nightclub anyway, whatever I'd been wearing. I'm sure he just wanted to see if he could make a girl spend damn near all the money she had, on a dress she didn't need, by the sheer force of his personality.

'Of course,' she goes on, putting out her cigarette and looking away from Imogen, 'of course, you're his mother and that makes it a lot more difficult. I'm sorry if it hurts you to hear this. But I guess you're right and in a way I must hate him after all. He made me so very unhappy.'

'That was a year ago.'

'No. No. He made me unhappy for always. That's what's so terrible.' She stands up, recollects herself, even manages a laugh: 'I wonder what happened to the cat.'

'Which cat?'

'Thomas's cat.'

'There was a cat?'

'Yes, Thomas's cat. It lived in his flat. It was a problem for me. I like cats, but I have some sort of allergy to them. When I told Thomas about it he just laughed and said to me, "Well then, I suppose we'd better have you put down, no?" I think he really loved that cat.'

Imogen picks up the photo of Tommy at the party. 'May I borrow this? You see, I came here without a picture of him. And maybe I'll need it.'

'Borrow it?' says Véronique. 'Why, have it, keep it. I don't want it anymore.'

'You kept it yourself, for a year.'

The girl shrugs. 'Some things you don't just throw out.'

They are in the hall. Then Imogen suddenly remembers the key, the landlady and the key. How she has to get into Tommy's apartment, how she has to find the landlady, how she has no idea where to ask, who the woman is, how Tommy never told her anything . . .

'I have a key,' Véronique says.

'What?'

'I said I have a key to his apartment.' Then, as Imogen stares: 'It's not so very extraordinary. He gave it to me when he went to Spain, so I could go water the plants, listen to the answering machine, that kind of thing. Then we stopped seeing each other, he never asked for it, somehow we just forgot about it. I guess it still works . . .'

She goes off into the room, reappearing a moment later with a small keyring. 'I can't remember which key goes with which lock. You'll just have to mess around. This little one, I know, is for the mailbox. Try it, anyway. You may find something.' She writes down a telephone number and tears it off the block of paper. 'Now you know where to find me. What's your hotel? Berlioz? Then I can call you if I think of anything.' She smiles awkwardly and, in fact, quite warmly. Really, the girl is not so bad.

It is an oddly anticlimactic farewell. Véronique opens the door and, as if on cue, Stéphanie emerges from inside the apartment, puts her arm round her friend's shoulder. Imogen pauses in the act of dropping the keys into her handbag and 'Are you going to go there straightaway?' asks Véronique.

'Why yes. Of course.'

Suddenly all the girl's bitterness is recollected. 'Go, then. Go and see. Go open Pandora's box.' The two girls watch her as she searches for, finds the light switch and starts off down the stairs.

Don't you know how we've all been worrying about you?

So, then, to Thomas's evidence.

It is a studio apartment of perhaps thirty square metres. There is a small entrance hall; off it, to the right, a tiny bathroom with shower, washbasin, lavatory. Ahead there is a kitchen, large enough to contain the usual oven, refrigerator, sink unit, cupboards, as well as a small formica-topped kitchen table and two chairs. To the left is the one largish room. The windows at the far end give onto the miserable courtyard whose opposite wall looms close. There is very little light. The room is furnished to a minimum. Below the window is a futon which can transform, apparently, into a sofa and two low tables. To the right of the bed the telephone is placed on top of the answering machine; to the left is a chest of drawers with bookshelves above. At the near end of the room, in a sort of recess, there is a large black wooden table, with two pliable wooden chairs. Another such chair stands against the near wall, next to the piano. A carpet of Chinese design covers most of the red tile floor. The walls are papered white. The windows are uncurtained.

The whole is incredibly dirty. Evidently this is less the result of personal neglect than of the sheer decrepitude of the building. Dust seems to drift from the corners, collect between the broken tiles of the floor. The wallpaper peels, yellow with cigarettes and with the pitiful light which penetrates the apartment. The carpet, of inferior quality, is already threadbare and stained with wine in several places.

The evidence of Thomas: a reproduction Klimt, a Russian anti-CIA poster, a framed advertisement from a fashion magazine. Some coffee-table books: Zille's pictures of Alt Berlin, Beaton photographs, a handsomely illustrated edition of Malory's *Morte d'Arthur*, several very expensive Italian fashion magazines. Cassettes, predominantly German late romantic music, Mahler's symphonies, *Der Rosenkavalier;* Rachmaninov, Puccini, a lot of Mozart, a little Bach; and then some Italian disco music and French light pop music. The books are mostly French: the complete Proust, the complete Flaubert, some modern novels from Gallimard, some detective stories; then *Teach Yourself Italian*, guides to Paris, a biography of Rilke, a few other things – surprisingly few books, considering how voraciously he once read. On the piano his music: some Ravel, some Chopin, Berg, Bach, studies, and Schumann's *Kreisleriana* open on the stand, poignant, inescapably significant, like the dinner plates set out on the Marie Celeste, or like the remains of that other feast, in Sallust's house, in Pompeii. *This* then was the last piece Thomas played before being somehow spirited away?

Don't you know how we've all been worrying about you?

There is no wardrobe in the apartment. A few jackets hang on the back of the door. In the chest of drawers she finds a few pairs of trousers, some shirts, socks, underwear. Were these all the clothes he possessed? She cannot remember how he dresses: did he even care much about clothes? There are two pairs of shoes and one pair of trousers gathering dust under the bed. Where is her old trunk that he took from England? Dimly she remembers having seen it, and sure enough she finds it in the kitchen, shoved under the table and up against the wall. With difficulty, for her hands are trembling and her arms quite weak, she pulls it out. It is heavy and its contents thud around inside. She looks around her, then begins opening the cupboards – plates, pans, glasses. Finally in a cupboard under the sink she finds a toolbox, takes out a hammer and a screwdriver, and sets to work on the padlock, appalled at the amount of noise it makes.

And what if Thomas were to walk in now? If he were to arrive and find her there in his apartment, breaking open his trunk, what would she find to say to him? Just as on that other occasion when she sat in the school sickbay, waiting to go to the hospital, her imagination deserts her, she feels only guilt and shame at what she is doing and at the prospect of worse to come – going through drawers, reading diaries, opening letters. With every crack of the hammer she feels Thomas's presence in the room and winces at her own ridiculous position. And it says something for the remarkable woman she is that she sets about this messy task with the same selfless and stoic determination that she brings to her painting and sculpture, no more flinching at the pathetic sordity of this than at the soiling of her clothes or the crumbing of her hands, her face, her hair, with paint and clay. And this total unconcern for her own dignity is, paradoxically, her richest source of it, since true dignity always and by its very nature precludes a conscious recognition of itself.

So, were he to walk through the door now, sooner than reveal the real extent of her distress, she would cling to her own shame at being caught breaking into a trunk or ransacking a drawer full of letters, would be relieved to bear his anger or scorn, for in any case his liking or disliking her has long been irrelevant; and any such anger or scorn as he might show, transitory and, somehow, cosily normal, would at least permit them to carry on as before, she placed slightly in the wrong by this excess of maternal anxiety, he no more thoughtless and inconsiderate than many another boy of his age. Sooner this than acknowledge the gulf between them.

And in this way she would recover him, and recover the picture of the life they have had so far. Were Tommy to walk in now, all it would take from her would be a shamefaced smile, a few hackneyed and half-hearted reproaches – 'Don't you know how we've all been worrying about you?' – and the whole thing would be restored, they would be as they were before the telephone rang on and on in the empty apartment, before Tommy came to Paris, before even that night when the headmaster called up to tell her that Tommy, *her son*, had swallowed an overdose and been taken to hospital. Her will to have him back would be stronger than his will to move on; and she would do it, unflinchingly, humiliate herself before him if only he should not see her first flash of appalled recognition as he walks through the door.

Of course, Thomas does not walk in and the trunk contains only books and fleamarket pictures and a huge old typewriter. There are also some posters, El Greco, Caravaggio, Raphael. She feels a glow of pride at Tommy's unerring artistic taste: *her* gift. There is a French Monopoly set, some sweaters, two volumes of the 1986 Paris telephone directory, a dozen other books, mostly in French, nothing very interesting. Apart from the pictures they mean nothing to her, there is nothing remotely evocative in the peculiar eclecticism of his possessions; on the surface so impersonal and yet, with a little imagination, as essential a part of his life as the conjunctions which coordinate a line of verse or the thread in a square of cloth.

On the desk there is a pile of letters written in French. At first she imagines they might be written by Tommy himself until she notices, at the end of the first, the name Paul. All the letters are signed with 'Paul' or 'P'. They are dated but without address, all written between January and April of this year. They vary in length from two sides to twelve, the big, rather too firm handwriting soon filling out these small grey sheets. One letter begins *Mon petit Thomas;* another, more urgently, *Thomas –*, but the rest dispense even with this small formality and launch breathlessly into the text. Frustrated, she pushes them aside.

Next she picks up his address book. Some people are listed by surname, others by Christian name. At least half the entries are for Paris: she is soon able to identify the eight-digit telephone numbers and the *arrondissement* codes. She looks up Véronique, listed under V, and Daniel, under S for Solomon, with his address in Paris and his parents' address in Hampshire. Then she looks up the names of other friends of Tommy's she remembers from England, but these are few. She finds the address and number of the Conservatoire and of Tommy's piano teacher, Madame Fiorenza di Biasi. She looks for family numbers and finds none. Instead there is a bewildering collection of incomprehensibly foreign names and streets in far-flung cities that lurk as immaterially on the edge of her consciousness and sound with as vaguely disquieting a resonance as the mythical names of Troy or Thebes or Babylon the Great: Klas Wikberg, København, Denmark; Rolanda Rebrek, Ljubljana, Yugoslavia; Mario Russo, Napoli, Italia; Karin Pinter, 1120 Wien, Austria. And so it goes: addresses in New York and San Francisco, in Rome and Venice, in Hamburg, in Moscow, in Valencia, in Budapest: there it is, Bánföldi, Tibor, Helsinki út 33, Budapest, Hungary, and a telephone number. Budapest: an hour earlier she would have been unable to say whether Budapest was in Hungary or in Romania. Tommy has never been to Budapest, has never mentioned Hungary or Hungarian friends, not to her. How has he come to know this person, how often has he sent letters to this address, called this number? Bánföldi, Tibor: what kind of name is that, a boy's, a girl's? For some reason this one name, this Bánföldi, Tibor, arouses all her fury, as if it represents all her ignorance, all her helplessness; resentment and fury against this unknown, faceless, ageless, sexless entity who is yet for Thomas a face, a voice, occupying a place in time and geography even unto the day they met and where: dear or at least significant enough for Thomas to preserve it beneath the hieroglyphics of this address book. Bánföldi, Tibor, existing all unawares of her in that far country: she wants suddenly to call up this person, this Bánföldi, Tibor, to interrogate this friend or acquaintance or whatever of Thomas's. But how should she call Budapest, how address this stranger, in what language? The sheer impossibility of ever learning anything more redoubles her fury against the name and its owner and against that other foreign city where

Don't you know how we've all been worrying about you?

Tibor Bánföldi, a boy of seventeen, lies sleeping in the late afternoon in his parents' apartment in a sinister, evil-smelling, brutally ugly housing complex in the forlorn industrial south of Budapest.

Now she begins to go through the drawers. The first thing she finds is a file stuffed with telephone bills, electricity bills, monthly receipts for the rent on the apartment, communications from the bank. In the next are documents relating to the Conservatoire and to his musical activities – details of competitions, festivals, scholarships, masterclasses. Then there is a box filled with letters from herself: she feels a swift embarrassment at the sight of her own hectic handwriting, so many pages covered late at night at the big kitchen table, so much extravagance and anxiety poured out to Thomas and now tied up with elastic bands and stored away in a box. She tries to picture him, still half-awake, skimming through and then carefully re-reading one of her letters as he sits there over breakfast. She even pulls one out and tries to read it as if it were written by someone else. How would they have seemed to him, her phrases? But it is like trying to catch sight of oneself in a mirror or hear one's own voice as it sounds to others.

Next there is a plastic bag with postcards and photographs. Some of the postcards are from friends and of such far places as Bali, New York, Stockholm. Their texts are generally jokey, revealing little. Then there are postcards that Thomas himself must have bought as souvenirs or for later use: daguerreotypes of classic French authors, some weird artistic shots of the Berlin Wall, some postcards of Madrid, Granada, Barcelona – she feels a sick pang as she handles these – others of Italy, Biarritz, small Breton villages. There are only a few photographs: Tommy posing with a cigarette on the terrace of a café that could be anywhere in Europe;

Tommy with his arms round two girls in front of Notre Dame; Tommy asleep on a coach with a big coat covering his body. There is a photo of Véronique, smiling. A photo of a teenage boy with long brown hair standing on a railway station. A photo of herself taken some ten years before.

She looks again at the photograph of Thomas on the café terrace. There are two cups on the table, two packets of cigarettes, someone else's jacket draped over the empty chair. Again she notices, in a detached and regretful way, that her son is quite beautiful.

The telephone rings. Her first crazy thought is that this is Tommy calling. She stares at the phone, which rings six times, then there is a single short ring as the other hangs up. Its echo persists in the silence until she is able to hear her own heart beating, the blood in her ears. A few seconds pass, then even as she stares the ringing starts again, this time as it were even more imperative, more interrogatory, for a full unbearable minute.

Like a criminal or a child caught out at some wrongdoing, Imogen gathers up letters, diary, address book, and lets herself out of the apartment.

He answers with the unmistakable alacrity of one who has been waiting by the phone. 'Ah, I am happy that you call. I have been thinking about you.'

'Have you found the boy? Thierry?'

'I am afraid, no. I will try. Have you found your son?'

'How do you — ?' She stops. She is thinking furiously. Then: 'You said you would help me. Can we meet?'

Now she waits for him on the huge *parvis* of the hôtel de ville, much traversed by skateboarders. Normally careless of her remarkable appearance, tonight she has remembered to pull out the one dressy item in her luggage, a beige jacket with calf-length skirt, packed as an afterthought, has re-done her lustrous hair and even clasped a gold bracelet around her wrist. Her handbag, habitually empty of combs, lipsticks, all feminine impedimenta, is heavy now with Tommy's diary, address book, and the dozen or so letters which seem to acquire as she stands there a figurative weight by their unfathomable and loaded mystery.

She is of course a full fifteen minutes early. A quartet of American backpackers ask her to take their picture against the inspired folly of the hôtel de ville, which she does with the inexpertise of one who dislikes all inherently useless machines and furthermore despises photographs as a debased and encroachingly popular art-form. There follows an extended leave-taking as they repeat their thank-yous with smiles white and wondrous as if it were a miracle indeed to happen on another English speaker there in the teeming streets of Paris.

And then he is here, twenty-one years old, glowing darkly in the evening light, his eyelashes absurdly long, his hair exaggeratedly thick and shiny, his tan oppressively uniform and teeth intimidatingly white and regular – so she characterises the individual features of the boy smiling before her, refusing to invest with the slightest interest this face which, had she encountered it on some swarthy Sicilian shepherd way up a remote and extinct volcano, might well have sent her scampering off to her brushes.

He inclines and kisses her hand. Already she feels ridiculed. 'Let us go.'

'We can find a café.'

'Oh but no. We must have dinner properly.' He takes her arm and they walk along the quays, then cross the

Pont d'Arcole and down as far as the Tour d'Argent. 'Unfortunately we are not dining here,' he says with rehearsed and rueful humour. They walk the buckled streets of the Left Bank. 'Are you a student?' she asks. 'Not likely!' he retorts, such dusty prep-school English bizarre and charming in his accent.

As they walk he talks to her a little about Thomas. 'I didn't want to tell you at once, I didn't want to raise your hopes. I never knew him well, I knew him by a friend of mine, Thierry, who also has disappeared, it seems. I met Thomas only a few times, though we talked a lot those times we met. I had heard of him, of course, before I met him.'

'What?' demands Imogen. 'What had you heard?'

An unnecessary pause elapses before quietly and ingenuously he replies: 'Why, that he plays very well the piano, of course.' They turn up a miniscule, impossibly picturesque side-street, manoeuvring between the cars. 'Thierry took me to a party at his place . . . Thomas's place. Thomas was going with a French girl who has an American mother. I was introduced to Thomas, however, we did not speak much on that occasion, for the reason that he was the host and was occupied with his guests. You know the girlfriend, the half-American girl?'

'We've met only once,' says Imogen. 'Today in fact.'

'She is very nice,' he shrugs. 'I met Thomas second time, at Thierry's house. They were going away on a holiday, I think to Spain.'

'Who is this Thierry?'

Pierre smiles very slowly. 'Thierry? He is an actor – *enfin,* he would like very much to be an actor. He used to work as a waiter, in that bar, in fact, where by the purest chance we met last night. He is an old friend of mine. You wish to know I suppose how he took up with Thomas. Well, it was I think the time when Thomas wanted very much to be with French people, only French people, and Thierry wanted very much to be with English people, in fact with Americans, because he believed he was not going to have any success as an actor in France. And I remember that I told him it was very unlikely that Thomas knew any film producers in America or indeed anybody connected with the acting world in America *or* England, but it was no good, he was very enthusiastic about Thomas, and for a time they were together always.'

'Was Thierry a friend of Véronique?'

'Oh *no*,' he breathes in a rather old-maid, scandalised way. 'I do not think she liked him *at all*. We are here,' he says, steering her in through the door of a charming, three-storey, slightly askew old house on the top of the hill. 'I have booked!' he declares.

So they eat dinner in an intimate restaurant on the Mont Sainte-Geneviève where a variety of whisperly attentive waiters serve them with abundant portions of really very delicious foods none of which, naturally, succeed in exciting Imogen's slightest interest. 'I have these letters,' she announces, fishing in her bag. 'I found them in his apartment, on his table, this afternoon. I think they may be important. But I don't understand a word; they're all in French. That was why I phoned you, really. I want to know what they say.'

'Oh, you English,' he mocks gently, 'with your detective stories and your clues.' But he takes the letters even so, flicks through them, his playful expression darkening on certain phrases, his attention fixing deeper and deeper until he looks up and asks, quite sharply: 'You say that you found them in his apartment?'

'Yes, on the table, the desk.'

'Do you have any idea who they are from?'

'No,' says Imogen. 'Why? Do you?'

He looks at them again, moving the front sheet to the back, the front sheet to the back, as if checking a pack of playing cards. Then: 'No,' he says. 'No, I don't.' He sets them down. 'Listen,' he commands, then seems at a loss to continue, begins to read again, passing his tongue over his lips, while Imogen stares at him, held by that 'Listen' as by the raised baton of a conductor.

Finally she insists: 'What is in these letters?'

He looks around uncomfortably. 'Thomas never spoke to you about a man named Paul?'

'No. Did he to you?'

'Not explicitly. These letters are from a man named Paul. He must have been some kind of friend of Thomas. I say man rather than boy because they are the letters of a man. They are rather disturbing, these letters. I think this man was very attached to Thomas.' Now he looks at her: 'Are you sure you want to know what is in them?' He holds up his hand at her quick and violent reaction: 'Do not be nervous. I ask only because you may be shocked by what they say, and because it may be they are of no importance.'

Imogen says: 'I've told you, I found them on the desk, right there on his desk. And one of them – you see?' She takes the pile of letters and locates one in particular. '– is dated thirteenth of April, exactly the time when Tommy's answering machine went off, exactly the time when he disappeared. *How* can they not be important?' She tosses them down once more in front of him. 'Now please. I am asking you. Tell me what is in those letters.'

He gives a deep sigh. 'So be it.' He clears his throat and begins to read. And this is something like the text of the letters:

Don't you know how we've all been worrying about you?

> Call me, you said. You do not answer my calls, no more my letters. Do you have an idea how many messages I have left on that accursed machine of yours? How many hours spent waiting, waiting for you to answer? I am in no doubt that you are having far too good a time with those *charming* friends of yours, but such wanton carelessness has, believe me, lost all its charm . . .

> I could ruin you. I could ensure that you never study in Paris again, that you never obtain an audition, your so-called career would be finished, I could drive you out of France if I wanted. But I would not stoop so low for you. And I ask myself besides whether you would even care, so utterly and insolently have you ignored my offers and efforts to help you . . .

And again:

> When I think of what I have endured from you these last few months I am overcome by a feeling of intensest shame, which must be to your great satisfaction. At first I ascribed your behaviour to the callousness of youth, but now I see you as incredibly old, far older than I could ever be, and immeasurably cunning. I see now that as far back as Italy, when we sat on that café terrace in Verona, you foresaw this moment . . .

Pierre looks up swiftly, the attendant host. 'You are not eating.'

'Neither are you,' she says.

'I am translating,' he says with a smile. And indeed he is warming to the task, his brow darkening less from unease at revealing the content of certain passages as from the effort of rendering it properly, of searching out the exact word. While it is obvious that he is still skipping certain sentences and censoring certain words out of delicacy, she sees also his youthful enjoyment of the exercise. And, with a growing suspicion that his English is just a little bit better than it sounds, it occurs to her that if he is an actor he is as yet an imperfect one. There are little flaws of technique and moments of doubt which recall school concerts she has attended, those of her children and of their friends, where, groomed, drilled, dinner-jacketed, loftily bowing, immaculately professional, a sudden hesitation or nervous smile is enough to remind one that the performers are in fact only fourteen or fifteen years old.

> Do I have to remind you that you sought me out and not the contrary? Now you distance yourself, or hide behind a web of lies. So: you were ill on Thursday evening. And were you then too ill to answer the phone? Too ill to call up yourself and tell me you weren't coming? You play games with people, you play games all the time. And I must assume that you derive some satisfaction from the spectacle of misery you cause. But I warn you, your games are dangerous, and the next person may react quite differently to being treated as you have treated me. Believe me, I myself have entertained violent thoughts on more than one occasion . . .

> I have to congratulate you. You have been very adept at acquiring all sorts of knowledge which you now seek to use not only against me, but against those friends of mine whom in my thrall and folly I made the mistake of allowing you to meet. Don't think I am unaware that you are behind it all: that boy you sent along, and whom I must suppose to be some kind of friend of yours, is a very poor actor and certainly not intelligent enough to have taken the initiative alone. Remember that if now I am in the

> depths it was you who conducted me there, abusing all the love and tenderness which I felt for you and which could not have been more misplaced . . .

And finally, most terrible of all:

> I love you. I still love you in spite of what you have done, in spite of what you are. You are a part of my life now, for better or worse, and though I do not expect to touch a chord of that non-existent tenderness in your heart, I want you to know that I at least am incapable of hate, and that the words I spoke to you all those months ago in Italy are still true. All the more abject, then, that you should have sent along that terrible boy in your place, that thug, whose only thought . . .

He says, suddenly embarrassed: 'There's a lot more, much the same.'

Now she is interrogating him about the letters. 'I can't believe it. I really can't. Who on earth could have written such things?' She looks across at him. 'Really, you have no idea who this man Paul is?'

He moves uncomfortably in his otherwise comfortable chair. 'How should I? I told you already that Thomas and I were not close. But I do know —' He pauses.

'What?'

'I do know that Thomas had some very rich and influential friends. Not just in music, though mostly there of course, but in the TV, press . . . I cannot tell you who; he was very secretive about it, even with Thierry, I think. Maybe he was a little bit scared —'

Imogen thinks out loud: 'That's what Daniel said.'

'Daniel? Who is this?'

'Oh, a friend of Tommy's from school.' Pierre shrugs

his ignorance. 'This Thierry. Do you think that's who he could have been talking about, in the letter? He mentions an actor: "He is a very poor actor". Do you think that could have been Thierry?' – taking the words quite literally even though she has mentally called Pierre an actor only a few moments before.

'Perhaps,' he says, his fine face shuttering. It seems to her that he is thinking very hard. Then, suddenly rousing, he reaches across the table and touches her elbow gently. 'You're upset,' he says. 'You're trembling.'

'It's nothing.' She flinches excessively at his touch as from an electric shock. 'It's nothing. I'm just worried, that's all.' But his words so pronounced have released precisely the reaction they name, just as no words are so guaranteed to make you cry as 'Please don't cry': in naming her distress he has made it impossible for her to dissimulate that distress, has shown her brave façade for what it is. She feels that this boy opposite her, this foreigner her son's age, is her only ally, so readily do we construe as a willingness to help what is no more than that curious respect which the spectacle of suffering arouses in those who do not themselves habitually suffer. Shaking her head, looking down at the table, she says: 'I really should be getting back.' She reaches for her handbag, blinks around for a waiter.

Pierre holds up his hand. 'It is paid.'

As they walk to the taxi he says: 'I understand you. It is impossible to see the Thomas of these letters as the Thomas we know. They are obviously the letters of a madman.'

Imogen glances up at his handsome profile. 'You think so?'

'But yes. It is quite clear. Perhaps more so to me than to you. In French the letters are quite insane. Perhaps I could not show this as I translated them.

And the handwriting also, it is the handwriting of a madman.' He explains: 'I am very interested in these things, graphology and so on. Thomas also, by the way. Perhaps you think it is stupid, but – I have made a little study of this subject and I can tell you without hesitation. Those letters are disturbing. Disturbing and disturbed,' he adds, with a quiet and uncharacteristic precision which is itself disturbing.

'I'm sure you're right.' Then: 'He must be mad. He threatened Tommy. Do you remember? He threatened Tommy with violence.'

'Ah no,' says Pierre with an infuriating regard for literal truth, 'that is not quite so. He says only that he has had violent thoughts about Thomas. That is not quite the same thing as a threat.'

In the taxi they do not speak. Pierre glances at her from time to time in a concerned, reassuring way. When they arrive he puts his finger under her chin for a moment and lifts her face to his own, making a little questioning sound in his throat which, were it rendered into speech, would give something like: Now are you going to be all right? No one, as far as she can remember, has taken such liberties with her. He insists on accompanying her to the lobby of the hotel where sits installed the same receptionist as greeted her on her arrival. Imogen quite forgets to thank him for his time, his help, for the materially superb dinner she has, moreover, quite failed to enjoy, so surprised is she when he lifts her hand to his lips, kisses it gallantly, and murmurs a few words in Italian, words which mean nothing to her but which the receptionist evidently, from her expression, understands clearly. This time Imogen does not ask for a translation, and, as Pierre withdraws and she herself retreats, she feels the receptionist watching her in a slightly new way.

Tommy's circle

Tommy's Conservatoire is about five minutes' walk from his house, in a quiet street near several main thoroughfares, in a light, airy, graceful building quite at odds with this district of pornographic cinemas, delapidated hotels, and sinister abandoned boutiques of children's clothing where the naked mannequins, four feet tall, stand indecently around in shop windows like an invitation to a debauch. As she waits in reception she can hear, away and above, scales on pianos, a wind quintet practising, a soprano's warm-up exercises. The coffins of double basses stand in a corner. Students swing past with flute cases, violin cases, sheaves of music. On the wall are notices announcing master-classes in Marseille, scholarships to Basle, competitions in Madrid, summer courses in Ontario, and the students are of similarly international range, being variously French, Hispanic, Oriental, Scandinavian in appearance.

This is not the Conservatoire as she imagined it, on the rare occasions when she imagined it at all, as when for example Tommy first won her over to the idea, or when his early phone calls home were filled with his excitement at entering it. She pictured a sunlit building of glass and crystal, surrounded by rolling gardens or else close up against the meandering Seine, where grave and charming youngsters frozen in some eternal nineteenth century bent their reverent heads over keyboards or 'cellos, or sat in some hushed, porcelain tea-room to discuss Mozartian form; where their gesture towards a social life consisted in planning group trips to the opera or forming chamber ensembles; where the teachers were demi-gods from time to time descending to offer words infinitely wise and wonderful, rather than cynical engineers plugging away in this dusty, workaday, often thankless factory to discipline and inspire hard-edged and jaded adolescents, distracted by sexual and financial worries, into some semblance of effort or enthusiasm.

A word about Imogen and music. Though all four of her children are musicians and set on musical careers it cannot be said that Imogen often listens to music, much less enjoys it, if one is to go by the expression of acute agony on her face as she listens to, say, Tommy giving a recital in the Haslemere Municipal Library, or Toby leading the junior orchestra at school. In fact she rarely goes to concerts unless it is to hear her own children, and then only to sit there with her eyes fixed on the floor experiencing the renewed birth-pangs of proxy stage fright, or glaring at anybody in the audience who is irreverently whispering – something she does quite well, since she has terrifying eyes. After the concert she may talk with eclectic expertise of Tommy's cadenza or Vicky's solo, but all the while she remains predominantly aware that this is her son Tommy and her daughter Vicky, and not two young people aspiring after and on occasion reaching something rather more significant than a perfectly executed arpeggio or flawlessly sustained trill. And it is one of the ironies of her life that she, who has accompanied him to and sat through scores of auditions, who has never missed a concert of his if human agency permitted her to be present, and who in her own home has kept vigil over thousands of hours of practice – she has never really heard Thomas playing the piano.

No: Imogen loves music rather as it might be said a bird loves nature, if nature can be represented by such details as the worms with which it feeds, and the trees producing the twigs with which it furnishes a nest for its young. In this way her attitude is entirely instinctive and personal, a composer's worth being determined according as he treats her offspring. Thus she is profoundly grateful to Chopin, for example, for providing Thomas with so rich a repertoire, feels towards Bach rather as towards some benign uncle who has generously bequeathed Toby the splendid set of violin sonatas and partitas. She has little time for Tchaikovsky, bears a real resentment against Puccini and Wagner who squandered their talents in the opera house, and altogether fails to recognise the existence of someone like Monteverdi who committed the oversight of being born into an era when instrumental music was not as yet a going concern. This said, in so far as she is knowledgeable about music it is names and places which constitute her knowledge, names, institutions, prizes and positions, names resonant with power and influence. As to the works themselves, she is less interested in their creators than in the people who teach, perform, package and promote them, since it must be admitted that Beethoven, for all his undisputed genius, is no longer in a position to provide real practical help in furthering her son's career.

After a long while the woman returns. 'But your son is no longer with us, Madame Holm.' For a split second Imogen hears the words as the ghastly euphemism by which they serve in Anglo-Saxon countries, imagines that this woman is calmly announcing Tommy's death. She stares open-mouthed until the woman's next sentence elucidates her meaning as having been quite banally literal – '*Il n'est plus chez nous.* He has left the Conservatoire.'

The shock of this is scarcely less. 'This is nonsense,' announces Imogen.

The Gallic shrug.

'I mean,' says Imogen, 'how can this be? He's left? What do you mean? When?'

'In February, according to our records. He took his examinations at the end of January. A few weeks later we received from him a letter announcing his withdrawal from the Conservatoire.'

'This letter: do you have it?'

The woman raises her hands to heaven. 'Madame Holm, this is *absolutely* not my responsibility. I have only this information which I give to you. If the letter is to be found it is with the Director of Admissions, Madame Holm.'

'And where is he?'

'He is at a conference in Cologne.'

Imogen is thinking hard, her mind searching after straws to clutch at, as if by raising the objections of common sense which protest, for example, that a talented young music student does not simply throw up a scholarship place at a prestigious French conservatoire, she might somehow reverse the course of time and prevent Thomas from doing just this. 'And his scholarship, what about that? What about the money?'

'Ah, yes, there,' says the woman, pragmatic and Parisian, 'are one or two things to be clarified. I do not know what arrangements your son has made with the bursar of the Conservatoire. I know however that according to our records your son is still liable for payment of tuition fees for the second semester of this year, as his withdrawal from the Conservatoire was received only after the official opening of the new semester. According to our records this sum has still not been paid. When will you see your son, Madame Holm?'

'I don't know,' says Imogen. 'As soon as possible, I hope. I am still trying to locate him.'

The woman gives a pained and worldly smile. 'Perhaps then when you do you will remind him about this sum?'

Defeated, Imogen prepares to leave. Then, suddenly remembering, she turns back. 'And what about Fiorenza di Biasi? Where can I find her?'

'She was your son's teacher? Excuse me, I will take a look.' She pulls out a book, some sort of register, and murmuring over to herself 'Di Biasi, di Biasi', flicks over the pages. 'Ah, you are fortunate. Madame di Biasi is here today. She is teaching. She will be free in' – squinting up at the clock – 'approximately fifteen minutes.'

'Where is she teaching?'

'In Room 17. But' – suddenly alarmed – 'you may not go there. She will be free in fifteen minutes . . .'

But Imogen has already set off through the swing

doors and down the corridor, determined to confront this di Biasi woman and to find out what, just what, induced Tommy to leave the Conservatoire; what, just what, went wrong. As she strides down the dim, institutional passageways she scarcely notices the students who stand and chat in twos and threes, or hurry from one class to the next, but they notice her, this extraordinary figure, so misplaced, bizarre and somehow so striking in appearance, her whole consuming will bent on her son as she strides their corridors – they notice her and flinch out of her way as she passes, until the moment when she rounds on one, a bespectacled boy of about twenty, and demands in English: 'Where is Room 17?', to which he replies with that stammering and prudent politeness we would reserve for an alien landed on earth who required without further ado to be taken to our leader.

There is a small window in the door of Room 17 and she presses against it. At the far end of the really quite long and airy room a girl is playing on a grand piano. Nearby, another girl and boy of much the same age sit on two of the chairs placed all around the edge of the room. On the other side of the piano sit two women of middle age, a thickset grey-headed woman with a red face, and a neat small blonde in a black trouser suit and much costume jewellery. Occasionally the girl breaks off playing and speaks, the other two students speak, the little blonde woman speaks in a high voice, punctuating her remarks with jabs of her cigarette, and the ruddy, mannish woman adds a sort of counterpoint an octave lower. Then the girl starts playing again.

Imogen leans against a table in the corridor and battles with her impatience, eyes closed. And it is of course a full half hour before the class ends. The two girls leave first, chasing off to another appointment, then comes the little blonde woman, absurdly small between her hefty companion and the willowy boy. They are deep in discussion. Imogen steps forward and says: 'Madame di Biasi?' – not even sure which woman to address.

The little blonde woman smiles up at her with large blue eyes and thickly painted pink lips. '*Oui?*'

'Excuse me for bothering you like this, I'm Imogen Holm, Thomas Holm's mother.'

Mme di Biasi's smile fades but a fraction. She reaches out a fantastically beringed hand. '*Mais c'est un plaisir totalement inattendu, je suis ravie.*'

'I'm sorry, I don't speak French,' says Imogen. 'I wondered if we might have a word.'

Mme di Biasi addresses a few words to her companion, who nods. Then she turns to the boy, who has been listening to this exchange with altogether unconcealed curiosity. He smiles agreement, murmurs some farewell, and sets off down the corridor. Mme di Biasi beams up at Imogen. 'What is it that I can – euh – do for you, Mrs Holm?'

Imogen plunges in. 'I'm looking for my son Thomas. He was your pupil. I don't know where he is. He seems to have disappeared. I haven't heard from him in weeks. I just spoke to a woman who works here. She said he has left the Conservatoire. I don't understand. I wondered if you knew what had happened to him. I'm rather worried.'

Mme di Biasi is one of those people who express their bewilderment by the breadth of their smile: the more total the incomprehension, the more dazzling the smile. She looks up at the other woman who says something to her in French. Then, to Imogen, by way of explanation: 'Bernadette, my friend, speaks very well English. I do not speak so well this language. She will have to help me.' She pauses for a moment, looks around. 'We can go into this room for a few moments. Please follow me.'

They go back into the classroom, multiplied by the mirrors all around. Mme di Biasi seats herself elegantly at the piano, as if by right, with Imogen on one side of her and this Bernadette on the other, and at once takes out and lights a cigarette the ash of which she will proceed to flick onto the floor beside her petitely booted foot. 'Tell me, please,' she then says, 'in what way I may be of assistance to you, Mrs Holm.'

Imogen briefly recounts the purpose of her visit, pausing only when Mme di Biasi's smile becomes particularly intense, to allow her companion to interpret. Imogen asks: 'How long did he study with you?'

Mme di Biasi grinds out a cigarette with the toe of her boot and at once reaches for another. 'Oh, all the time he was at the Conservatoire. So, all of last year. In September I learned he had found another teacher, but still he came to classes with me. I do not altogether approve of students working with two teachers at one time, but it is the student's choice. Then in February I learned that he had left the Conservatoire. It was not a great surprise to me. I was expecting some such thing. And he was not regular at classes. I do not know what happened to him then. He never came to see me. We never met again.'

'Do you know *why* he left the Conservatoire?'

Mme di Biasi says with great tranquillity: 'Perhaps he felt that with his new teacher he no longer had need of the Conservatoire.'

'And who was this teacher?'

'Delamarche. Paul Delamarche.'

It is a second before Imogen makes the connection. '*Paul* Delamarche?'

'Yes, of course.'

'*Paul*?'

'Of course. Paul Delamarche.' Her smile sweetens.

I could ruin your career, Imogen remembers. *My offers and efforts to help you.* She asks now: 'Who is this Paul Delamarche?'

Mme di Biasi smiles up at the dust-swathed chandelier imperfectly centred above them. 'But Paul Delamarche is the greatest pianist in France. He is one of the greatest pianists in the world. You did not know?' Imogen is lost in furious calculation and Mme di Biasi glances up swiftly at her companion as if to verify that she has made her meaning clear to the Englishwoman. At a nod of assent from Bernadette she continues: 'I will confess that I was very surprised to learn that Delamarche had taken Thomas as a pupil. Delamarche is not a teacher, I mean, he does not ordinarily accept pupils. And Delamarche is the very best, he takes only the very best.'

'And Thomas?'

This time Mme di Biasi's smile is not prompted by incomprehension. 'Ah, Thomas is not of the very best.'

'What do you mean by that?'

'What I say. Thomas is a very good pianist, he has some talent, he was a good student who worked well for me and I was sorry that he left as I believe I could have taught him much.' She smiles up at Bernadette, who bends her eyes with twinkling affection on the piano teacher. 'He may have a fine career as an accompanist or a répétiteur with an opera company. *But.* He will never be a great pianist.'

'If he worked harder —' persists Imogen.

Fiorenza di Biasi waves her cigarette. 'It is not *work.* He *worked.* He worked quite hard enough. After a certain point it is not work which counts.'

Imogen, coldly: 'Perhaps Mr Delamarche thought otherwise.' She is piqued, thinks Imogen, she is resentful; behind that smile she has never forgiven Thomas for dropping her, and now she wants to denigrate his playing. To test this suspicion she asks: 'And what did you feel when Tommy left you?'

'I felt —' But she breaks off with a frown, turns to her companion and speaks rapidly for a moment. Bernadette explains: 'Fiorenza says that when a student decides to leave this is never a moment to question the student, but a moment to interrogate oneself. In that way one may learn something for the next such occasion.'

This is not good enough for Imogen, furious with the little woman for denying her son genius, and instinctively ascribing to spite her fatal and condescending judgements on Tommy's ability. 'What about this Delamarche? What do you know about him?'

'As I have said. He is the best. He is one of the greatest musicians in France.'

'I mean, as a person.'

'Ah, there —' says Mme di Biasi. Then, carefully: 'Paul Delamarche is a man of great intelligence and great integrity. You know, Mrs Holm, in our world it is not always easy to guard one's integrity. Paul Delamarche is one of those rare persons: a great musician *and* a great man. He has done' – she touches her forehead briefly – '*innumerable* good things. I give you only one example: it was he who conceived and organised the annual summer course in Nice which, by the way, Thomas your son attended last year. I believe it was there that they met.'

'It can't have been there,' says Imogen. 'Tommy didn't go.'

'Ah no?' says Mme di Biasi with great nonchalance. 'Ah well, I am wrong.'

'And do you know him well, this Delamarche?'

'No,' replies the other, simply. Then, outrageously, she begins to address Imogen in the following terms: 'You are very concerned for Thomas's success, and that is a good thing. But Thomas can fail too. Everyone has the right to fail. And if he fails it will not be his fault or your fault or the fault of anyone else, and it will be a sad and futile exercise to look around for the fault where there is none. Thomas has the right to fail, you must give him that right. Thomas is more than his successes. If you really want to help him you must take the failures along with the successes: people are made up of both. Thomas can fail, too.'

But this is the one idea which Imogen cannot countenance, Tommy's assured success being the cornerstone of her faith in life, the motivation and justification for everything she does and has done. Daniel's veiled insinuations are nothing beside the reasoned, deadly pronouncements of this little woman sitting and smoking on her piano stool; Véronique's ill-concealed bitterness has not one-tenth such power to affect her, no more than any other slur on his character or troubling revelation, subjective and temporal and easily incinerated in the furnace of her maternal love. But what is the long martyrdom of her marriage if Tommy can fail? What all her sacrifices and compromises? And what is the purpose of her abject and Sisyphean struggle with her own art all these years, the renunciation of her own fulfilment, if still Tommy can fail? Standing up she declares heatedly: 'I think it is *absolutely* outrageous of you to speak to me in this way. You have absolutely *no* idea of my relationship with my son and *no* place to comment on it. You can believe what you want to believe about Tommy. But don't put ideas into *my* head and words into my mouth. Who on earth do you think you're speaking to?'

She stands there in her breathless and shaken grandeur. As for Mme di Biasi, if she has not understood everything, the essence at least is clear, and, smiling with infinite calm, she says: 'You are quite right. I spoke – how shall I put it? – out of turn. I ask you to forgive me.' She pulls a small red notebook from her bag and scribbles a few words on it. 'As a gesture' – writing – 'of my good will, you will, I hope, allow me to help you. Here –' she folds and holds out the square of paper '– is Paul Delamarche's address and number. If he is in France, this is where he can be found.'

Reluctantly Imogen takes the paper – reluctantly, for to take it implies a forgiveness she is not yet ready to extend. She stands there a moment longer, torn between saying any number of things, then, with a sharp 'Thank you for your time', turns on her heels, still seething with anger and with a palpable sense of defeat, and leaves them. As she closes the door she hears the great piano teacher strike up a chord behind her, the better, as it were, to mark her exit.

She has one great recourse: the family. So she finds a Post Office and puts through a call to Haslemere and her daughter, Vicky, down for a few days from London.

'I've been chasing around for forty-eight hours. I hate this place, I can't speak their bloody language. Tommy lives in the most appalling corner of town, a kind of *souk*. I couldn't believe my eyes. He wasn't there of course. I've been to the Embassy, they were no help at all, needless to say. "Our functions are primarily diplomatic, Mrs Holm. Unless you have reason to believe that your son is in danger . . ." Of course I have reason to believe. Just try convincing them.'

'So what are you going to do now?' asks Vicky.

'God knows. I met Daniel – you remember? He's become terribly snooty and obviously doesn't give a damn whether Tommy's alive or dead. I met Tommy's girlfriend, yes, he had a girlfriend but it's over now, apparently. She's quite drab but at least she speaks English. Not that she had anything to say, she just spent half an hour running Tommy down for ditching her. She has no idea where he is. Then there was some awful friend of Tommy's who looks like a gigolo, I met him in a bar full of queers.'

'Mummy, I'm sure he'll turn up. Have you tried the Conservatoire?'

'Listen. This is the extraordinary part. Tommy's left the Conservatoire. After the Christmas break he just went back, did his mid-year exams, then wrote them a letter to say he was leaving. I met his piano teacher, an awful little woman. She had another woman with her, moustache, huge. Anyway, the point is she's obviously furious with Tommy for leaving her and so now she spends her time running down his playing. He goes to another teacher now, privately. She gave me the teacher's number but he's not there. There's something funny about the teacher. Listen, Vicky. Have you ever heard of somebody called Paul Delamarche?'

'Of course, everyone's heard of him.'

'Well, I hadn't, not until this afternoon. And there's another thing. You remember last summer, when we all thought Tommy was at the summer school in Nice? Well he wasn't. He was in Spain.'

'Perhaps he's there now then. Really, Mummy, I

don't see what you can do about it. If Tommy was in trouble you know he'd call. He's just gone on holiday or something and forgotten to tell you. You know how thoughtless he is. Oh – hang on a minute, David wants to speak to you. David's coming on.'

'Oh God,' says Imogen, David being her husband.

'When are you coming home, woman?' he roars down the telephone, not in anger but because he himself is slightly deaf and besides, there is the Channel between them. 'What good do you think you're doing the poor boy, gadding about Europe like this? There's a crisis here. Toby's been sent home from school.'

'Well, can't *you* cope with it?' she demands irritably, so long accustomed to being indispensable that it no longer affords her the slightest satisfaction.

'You know very well I can't. Somebody has to go up to the school and sort it out. I can't go, it's too far, I don't know these people. Stop worrying your head about Tommy. He's probably having an *histoire* with a Frenchwoman.'

Imogen sighs deeply. 'Give me Toby,' she commands.

'I can't, he's not here. He's gone up to London for a rock concert.'

'You let him go to a rock concert when he's been sent home from school?'

'There was nothing I could do, you know how he is. When are you coming home?'

'You stupid man!' hisses Imogen.

'What's that, Imogen? I can't hear you. The line's very bad.'

Imogen hangs up, her fury only partially relieved.

Imogen calls Paul Delamarche's number five times in the space of one hour, and five times it is engaged.

'How,' she enquires, 'can I get to Saint-Germain-en-Laye?'

The receptionist looks up from her paperback and removes her stylishly framed glasses. Each encounter between them seems a little frostier as Imogen stays on in Paris and there is no sign nor even evidence of a son. The girl carefully lays aside her novel before addressing herself to the guest.

At La Défense, the first disgorged army of office workers climbs onto the train. Dreary little suburbs open up, one after the other, their identical corner cafés, car showrooms, discount furniture stores, peeling Dubonnet posters. The shutters, the wrought iron balconies so compellingly picturesque in the city, here have a shabby and second-rate look. And now the grim university edifices of Nanterre. Then they cross the Seine and are all at once it seems in the country, with graceful white houses sheltered by orchards and set disdainfully back from the intrusive suburban railway which in the so recent past yoked these sedate and august former villages to the metropolis, the quietly delapidating weekend villas emptied, boarded up, repurchased by real-estate prospectors and resold to commuters seeking a garden and a little space for families that have outgrown their cramped and fume-clogged midtown apartments. At Chatou-Croissy, at Le Vesinet the businessmen of the combination-lock briefcases disembark and head for home.

The end of the line, Saint-Germain-en-Laye, graceful and costly suburb. Still smarting from her fury at the di Biasi woman, she doesn't at once go in search of Delamarche. A little way outside the station she finds herself in front of an alcoholic café, its picture windows blue with gathering dusk. A few men are sitting quietly over glasses of wine. Two others are playing dice at the bar. I could drink a glass of wine, she tells herself – she the abstinent, the self-denier. And the subtly corrupting breath of Thomas's circle and Thomas's city unfurls from the tavern door, like some perfume or High Church incense.

By the time she leaves, an hour later, it is dark outside. Fuddled by the wine, she pulls out her map and locates the street once more, a mere two minutes' walk from the station, near to the now skeletal market place, beautiful houses alongside bijou boutiques straggling along either side. Coming closer she is aware through the gentle buzzing in her head of an unusual amount of activity ahead of her, uncommon numbers of people in the street, noises and lights, centred on that part of the street where she dimly calculates Delamarche's house to be, centred there with a kind of disastrous inevitability, and, for her, with the horrible sense of having lived this before.

'This isn't real,' she tells herself. 'This isn't what I came for.'

Someone is shouting to the others to stay back, stay back. She pushes closer between two men in overcoats. As she watches, a shape is brought out of the house on a stretcher, a boy of maybe twenty with longish hair climbs after it, the doors of the ambulance slam. The same metallic voice shouts a command and the female silhouette in the doorway withdraws, the light in the hallway shutting off after it.

Beyond the incomprehensible words

Next morning.

'Allo, oui?'

'I'd like to speak to Mr Delamarche, please.'

'Yes, this is Mrs Delamarche speaking.' An American voice.

'Yes, I'd like to speak to Mr Paul Delamarche, please.'

'Who is this, please?'

'Mrs Holm. Mrs Imogen Holm.'

A slight pause. 'I'm sorry, but – just who *are* you?'

'My son is a pupil of your husband's. Thomas Holm. I am his mother —'

'Where are you speaking from?'

'Paris. The Hotel Berlioz —'

The voice breaks in, raw with jaunty hysteria. 'Well, you will be pleased to hear, Mrs Holm, that at this precise moment no one can say whether my husband is going to live or die, not me, not the doctors at the hospital, not anyone. Given the circumstances, this was perhaps not the best moment to make contact.'

'I'm terribly sorry,' says Imogen, 'I had no idea . . .'

'And what *I* would like to know,' goes inexorably on the voice, 'is: don't you think your family has done enough damage already? Isn't it really time you left us alone?'

'*My* family?' says Imogen. 'Why on earth —?'

'When next you speak to that son of yours, would you convey these sentiments? Goodbye, Mrs Holm.' And then the purr of the dialling tone.

Now she is sitting with Diane, Mrs Delamarche, in the lobby of the Hotel Berlioz. It is late in the afternoon and they have had coffee brought through to them from the kitchen.

Mrs Delamarche is speaking in her soft, international voice. 'You understand, I was in a terrible state this morning, that's why I was so rude to you. Yesterday evening, and then all last night I didn't sleep, and then this morning in the hospital. You can understand how I felt. And believe me, Thomas Holm was the last name I wanted to hear at that particular moment.'

Diane Delamarche is in her mid-thirties, a smart, good-looking woman of tailored appearance with lustrous blonde hair set up in a loose bun. Canadian, not American. Although the circumstances are perhaps too exceptional to allow generalisation, she looks rather like a woman who does not smile often. She looks, she talks, business-like and well trained, as if she would make a good lawyer or personal assistant, whereas in fact it transpires that she had ambitions to be a musician before realising that she was not sufficiently talented and then moving into concert management, in which sphere she met her husband, the failed suicide of last night.

Imogen found her waiting there in the lobby on her return from another abortive trip to Tommy's apartment. A youngish, well-dressed woman waiting in one of the armchairs: Imogen could not understand why this woman should be watching her, should be staring quite openly. Then, at the desk, asking for her key, the receptionist told her with strident foreknowledge: 'This lady is here to see you, Mrs Holm.'

'I'm sorry,' she said, standing up, coming forward. 'My name is Diane Delamarche, we spoke on the phone this morning. I came here to . . . well, rather, to explain.'

Now it was Imogen's turn to stare. 'Paul Delamarche's wife . . .?'

'That's right.'

'Your husband —?' And then stopped.

'Out of danger,' breathed Diane, although Imogen's question would in fact have been quite different.

Imogen looked around rather helplessly, at the empty lobby, at the receptionist, until Diane took the initiative and asked the girl, in English: 'Could you please send through to the kitchen for some coffee for us?'

Now they sit, discussing Paul, and Imogen thinks how extraordinary it is that Diane should be here, in this hotel, in that chair, so scrubbed, so tailored, after a husband's near fatal overdose and a night without sleep and constant coming and going between hospital and home.

'He was stomach-pumped. He was out of danger in the early hours of this morning. Before you called, in fact, though I didn't know it at the time. One of the reasons I was so nervous was that I was waiting to hear from the hospital; I wanted to keep the line free. I was sitting by the phone. There was no damage, once the poison was out of him. I told them he was better off at home. They didn't want to let him go. I persuaded them. They wanted him to talk to some damn hospital psychiatrist. As if that would do any good. That would have been the worst thing. I had to argue and argue. The French! I persuaded them to let me take him home this afternoon.'

'And where is he now?'

'At home.'

Imogen exclaims: 'But then shouldn't you be . . .?'

'Oh, don't worry. His son is with him, Paul's son. Paul *was* married before, you know. He has two children.'

'But a *child* . . .' says Imogen.

'Simon is twenty-one,' says Diane. 'Don't worry. He's probably better with Paul than I am myself at the moment, I'm so hysterical —' Although she looks nothing of the kind. 'Simon went with him to the hospital; he was there the whole night. I couldn't have gone there, I'd have gone crazy. Just to think that Paul could *do* that, that he could be so desperate . . .' Suddenly she lets her face fall into her hands, and Imogen notices that the hands are shaking.

Imogen leans forward in her chair, reaches out her own hand which remains there, in the air, touching nothing, as near as she can bring herself to go. It doesn't seem real to her, this problem, doesn't seem right that *anyone* should have a problem, anyone else: she feels an indefinable resentment mixed in with the statutory pity. She says: 'I understand how you must be feeling. Believe me. I know. Tommy, when he was at school, did the same thing . . .'

Diane looks up sharply from her hands, tight-lipped

with near total contempt. 'I hardly think it's comparable,' is all she says.

Then, ashamed of her sharpness, she begins to talk about Paul. 'He is not just anyone. He is not even simply a great musician. I don't say this only because he's my husband, *that* kind of pride means nothing, God, I know that. Ask anyone, anyone who knows anything about music, here in France, anywhere.' And Diane goes on to tell her that even outside his own specialist world he enjoys a certain celebrity as the man who persistently refused a prestigious and very lucrative contract with a particular record label because it would involve working with a German conductor who had long ago gained advancement through compromises to the Nazis. Other French musicians followed suit, until the whole affair had become a question of artistic and humanitarian honour. And wasn't it he who, in more recent times, when the news first came through of Ceausescu's fall, organised a pair of impromptu Christmas concerts the proceeds of which went, along with the fees of every participant, to the Romanian revolutionaries and all the oppressed of that country? If Diane is exaggerating when she calls Paul Delamarche the artistic conscience of his generation, nonetheless it is fair to say that he has earned a sort of authority in integrity few others can boast.

But Imogen, impatient and really rather confused by all this: 'Where does Thomas fit into the whole story?'

Diane sits back in her chair with the ironical smile once more on her face. 'I'm hardly the person to ask. I was hoping for some kind of answer from *you*. What has *he* told *you*?'

'Thomas is missing. Why do you think I'm in Paris?' As if the world should know.

'Missing?' Then there is a long silence, during which

Diane rubs her tired, tired, unslept eyes with the back of her wrist. 'Missing from where? I don't understand. Missing since when?'

And Imogen tells her something approximating the whole story: the answering machine, the postcard from Susan, her own trip to Paris and her finding the abandoned apartment. It is then that Diane asks something really quite pertinent and which no one has thought to ask before. 'Did he leave his passport behind in the apartment?'

'Why yes, as a matter of fact he did. I saw it in a drawer.'

'Then he can't have gone very far, can he? Or have been intending to.' She is bitter, as if regretful at offering any clue or assistance in the tracking down of Thomas.

'I suppose not.'

'And you –' says Diane, in quite a challenging tone of voice, 'if you haven't seen your son in all this time, what do you know about Paul? How did you come to be calling me up at eight o'clock this morning?'

Imogen explains carefully: 'There were his letters in the flat, a whole pile of letters, all from this Paul, all of them signed Paul. They were on his desk. I had no idea who Paul was. I didn't even know he was Tommy's teacher. Then, when I went to the Conservatoire, I was talking to Tommy's piano teacher – the first piano teacher, Fiorenza di Biasi – do you know her?'

Diane shrugs. 'The name.'

'– and she told me that Tommy's new teacher was called Paul. I had to assume it was the same. She gave me his address and telephone number – *your* telephone number. And I tried to call yesterday and there was no reply, and so yesterday evening — '

Diane looks up at her swiftly. 'Go on. Yesterday evening –'

'I was at your house,' Imogen says, 'I'd gone to see Paul. When I went up the street I saw the ambulance and so on . . . I went away.' Her voice tails off, she feels slightly ashamed of the whole enterprise, remembering the café, the glasses of wine, her lurching fear as she approached the house.

'And why was it so important for you to see Paul?'

'Because of what was in the letters.'

'And how do you know what was in the letters?'

'Somebody translated them for me.'

'Who?' she presses.

'A friend,' says Imogen, suddenly defensive. And in the face of this woman's interrogation she actually comes close to regarding Pierre as a friend, an ally, has a swift and warm feeling of protectiveness for him and gratitude toward him. But it is better to be honest: 'Actually, not a friend of mine. Somebody Tommy knew, a boy I met by chance in a bar.'

Diane leans forward, her eyes narrowed, her arms crossed, and asks: 'Which boy?'

All at once it is unnerving, complex and unnerving, that Diane might know Pierre. Imogen says in a deliberately throwaway voice: 'His name's Pierre, Pierre Saporito, I think. He's half-Italian, a student or . . .'

Diane laughs suddenly, very high, very long, a laugh out of all proportion to the circumstances, an uncalled-for laugh, so much more so since there is no amusement in it. Finally: 'A student!' she says. 'Oh, he's not a student. I know that boy. And what did *he* have to tell you about Paul?'

'Nothing,' says Imogen. 'He said . . . he says he doesn't know Paul.'

Diane shrugs: this is not worth the arguing.

'And then there was this,' says Imogen, reaching into

her handbag. This morning, after the telephone call to Diane, after piecing together some sort of idea as to what had happened, she went to Strasbourg Saint-Denis, to Thomas's building, and opened the mailbox. There was not much in there of interest: some bills, some circulars, some letters addressed to a previous occupant, a telegram sent by herself (two and a half weeks ago!) and this postcard from Paul. A photograph of a nail being driven through a hand. On the other side, five words in French and the signature. Paul. She stood there in the corridor of that dreadful apartment building, with her so recent knowledge of Paul, she looked at the blatant melodrama of the postcard and at the message from the man who was now in hospital, poised between life and death. And there was something wrong with it, something that disturbed her beyond the incomprehensible words. Now, with an unformed hope of clearing up this mystery, she hands the postcard to Diane.

'Oh yes, that's him all right,' she says. 'That's Paul.' She lets the postcard drop on the table between them, pushes her fist to her mouth, like a child. The receptionist looks up from her magazine. Diane sighs, drops her hands into her lap, and tries to compose herself.

'What is it?' says Imogen. 'What does it say?'

But Diane just sits there, immaculately dressed, serious, staring ahead, knowing far more than she tells. Suddenly she looks up, speaks to the receptionist in French. 'More coffee,' she explains to Imogen.

They are silent for a while, Diane staring ahead of her. And then Imogen realises that this woman, for all her poise, her elegance, her clothes, her remembering to order coffee from the hotel kitchen, is still deeply in shock. She says softly, in a voice so tender and hesitant that one might think sympathy were an astounding and unlooked-for discovery in her life: 'Can you help me? Do you know where Tommy might be?'

Diane blinks at her. Then, wearily: 'I'm sorry, I have really no idea where he is. You must understand, I didn't know him at all.'

'What do you mean?'

'I never even met the boy.' The boy. Then she explains: 'It's not so strange as it sounds. I didn't often meet Paul's pupils. I didn't want to. That was just another part of his working life. And I know now, and for what reasons, Paul didn't want me to meet Thomas, not at all. When they started there was nothing unusual. Paul has an apartment in the centre of Paris, not really an apartment – a studio – and that's where he usually gives lessons. It's more convenient. And from the beginning he didn't allow me to visit his studio, ever.'

Imogen smiles her scepticism.

'Oh no, I'm quite serious,' says Diane. 'You have to remember that Paul was forty when he married me, and he'd been divorced another eight years before that. He was out of the habit of being married, and he had his own habits, his own ways. I was the last person to want to interfere with that. My God, whatever made it work for him I was more than happy.'

'So you don't know Tommy?'

'I saw him once. He doesn't know that. Paul still doesn't know that. I think Paul went to some lengths to make sure we never met each other.' Diane narrows her eyes the better to remember. 'Sometime at the end of last year, when I knew that something was going wrong . . . that was when I saw him. Paul said he was going to adjudicate some competition in Germany, and I knew somehow, the way you do, that this wasn't true. And Paul, you know – he doesn't know how to lie even when he has to. It wasn't too difficult for me to find out that there was no competition going on in Germany.' She tells it all in an amused, anecdotal kind of way, as if she were obliging an interviewer with further evidence of her husband's artistic eccentricity. 'After that it didn't take much effort to find out that Paul had gone off to Italy. By then I knew there was something between him and this boy – Thomas – and I learned that Thomas, too, had suddenly decided to go off for a short "working holiday" to Italy. I found them easily enough. Paul doesn't know it to this day. I walked down a street in Verona which ended in a square, and there in the square, at a café table — ' She begins to speak very slowly, the light, bantering tone quite gone. 'They were sitting talking. I came down the street and I wondered, what will happen if I go up to them? I was curious as well: here at last was this Thomas. And I walked down to the edge of the square, and then . . . I walked away again. I'd seen everything I came for.' Now she is separating every word. 'I left them there,' she says, 'talking in that café in Verona. And to this day, they do not even know I was there in Italy with them.' She looks suddenly hard and long at Imogen. 'The most humiliating moment of my life,' she says.

'Excuse me.'

The receptionist is standing there, waiting to position the tray on the table between them. It offers them a moment of respite. Imogen leans back in her chair, Diane sighs, pushes a strand of hair back into place, then reaches into her bag for a carton of cigarettes and a lighter. 'Do you mind?' she says. 'I don't usually, I haven't really smoked in years, but, you know . . .'

Imogen then says: 'Let me get one thing clear. Are you blaming Tommy for what's happened?'

Diane looks unhappy. 'Oh, I don't know. Paul hasn't been . . . completely well for two years now, since before your son came into the picture. And Paul had been obsessed with pupils of his before, that was his way. He accepted so few, only the very special cases. They had to interest him personally. And sometimes he didn't know where to draw the line with that interest. I suppose it was almost inevitable how he reacted. But with Thomas there was something different. I mean – you have to understand – what I know I know by implication: Thomas was the first one that he'd never talk about, to me.'

'Was he –' there is no other way to say it: '– was he in love with Tommy?'

'No, no, it was just his way, it was just an obsession, no.'

'He said he was.'

'When? To whom?'

'In one of his letters.'

Again Diane has that expression of contempt. 'How can you be sure what's in those letters? That boy would be capable of telling you anything.'

Imogen takes a deep breath. 'Perhaps. But *you* believe it, don't you?' Diane does not reply. 'What *was* between them?'

'Oh no,' says Diane, suddenly prissily reticent, smoothing her blouse, brushing back her hair. 'Nothing of that. I'm quite sure of it. I mean, after all I am his wife, I would know . . .' Suddenly she falters: 'You know, Paul is a genius . . .'

'Please,' says Imogen sharply, 'I'm trying to find my son.'

Diane puts a handkerchief to her eyes for a moment, then smiles, nods. 'Of course. I'm sorry. Of course. Well –' very briskly '– maybe Paul can tell you for himself. He wants to see you.'

'*Paul* does?'

'That,' says Diane, 'is my principal reason for coming. Oh, I know, I wanted to apologise for the way I spoke to you this morning, I wanted to explain. And I was a little curious as well; I wanted to see what you could be like and find out what you were doing here. But really, it was for Paul.'

Imogen says: 'So he knows I'm here?'

Diane smiles. 'I wasted no time in telling him, you can be sure of that.'

She stares for a moment into her coffee cup. 'You said your husband hadn't been well for two years . . .'

'And?'

'Well,' says Imogen, 'do you think your husband might be – in some way – oh, I don't know, disturbed?'

'Just what do you mean?' says Diane.

'Well, in view of what's just happened. And you see, Tommy *is* missing. And Paul . . . I mean, he said some very strange things in those letters, how he'd had thoughts of violence, that sort of thing, and I wondered . . .'

Diane turns on her with heavy impatience: '*Oh* no, *oh* no. If that's what you're talking about, you can forget it. Paul, harm anybody? Whatever harm was done in that relationship came from the other direction, you can be sure of that. And besides . . .' A little softer: 'That postcard there: why on earth would he send a postcard to someone he had . . . hurt?' Diane drains her coffee and stands up. And so to business. 'Please go and see him tomorrow. I don't know what he wants from you, I don't like the idea, I don't imagine it will be very pleasant for either of you. But I'm not in a position to go making objections at this stage.' She pulls a piece of paper from her bag. 'He wants to meet you in the Crillon; it's a hotel, Place de la Concorde, at noon. In the reception, mind. Don't worry, I've written everything down for you.'

'But how will I know him?' asks Imogen, and is gratified to see the shock on Diane's face that somebody might conceivably not know her husband.

It lasts only a minute. 'Ask at the reception. *They* know him.' A pause. Then: 'Will you do this? Please?'

'Of course,' says Imogen, in her turn surprised that the woman should imagine her reluctant: if there is one man in Paris she wants to see tomorrow, at noon, it is Paul Delamarche.

'Well, then. If you change your mind between now and then, well – you have our number.'

'Oh, I want to talk to him,' says Imogen, standing up. 'Believe me I want to talk to him.'

Diane says: 'I have to go back. I've been out too long.' But she does not move to go. 'If – if we don't see each other again,' she says at last, 'well, I hope you find your son.'

'Thank you,' says Imogen, oddly moved that in spite of all, and with whatever conventional insincerity, the woman has said so. 'And thank you for coming to talk to me. I'm sorry . . .' But she breaks off, not quite sure what she should be sorry for: for bothering them, for being here in Paris, for having had the son she had? They look at each other for a moment, wanting so much from one another, the two adversaries, and yet so alike in their adversity: they examine each other with respect and with a necessary hostility.

Then Diane pulls on a scarf and goes home to her husband.

The other room

'I will meet you at Strasbourg Saint-Denis, near where Thomas lives, opposite the Porte Saint-Denis, in the café called La Lune, at eight o'clock,' announces Pierre.

'I don't know where that is; how am I expected to find it?' says Imogen. 'Couldn't we meet at my hotel or — ?'

'La Lune, Strasbourg Saint-Denis, at eight,' says Pierre, and hangs up.

It is quarter to six now. So, she should plan to arrive half an hour in advance, to scour that suppurating *quartier* for Pierre's café. *Regarde la lune, la lune ne garde aucune rancune*. But the days, the days and above all the evenings are long in Paris, when you are looking for your child.

She thinks about eating something, going maybe to

the Café de Milan one more time and ordering, say, one dish, without wine, just to pass an hour. Odd that in Paris, gastronomic capital, its streets seemingly lined with restaurants, she should feel obliged to stick to this one, expensive, mediocre, boulevard brasserie simply because it was there that she went on her first evening, and where the waiters are no more polite nor tolerant of her idiosyncratic and faltering English-French than they would be anywhere else, nor the multilingual menu any less bewildering. She sits down in the lobby and pulls out the guidebook and flicks through the restaurant section. But there are thirty pages of restaurants, and the simple act of selecting one at random would entail a tiresome cross-reference of addresses, then checking on the metro map to find the nearest station, then working out the route, where to change lines, and besides, the guidebook is two years old at least, suppose the restaurant has closed down or changed ownership or name, or is open only from seven? Never go abroad without knowing someone there, what gold there is in that conventional wisdom. If only she had come to Paris before, with Thomas to prepare a schedule for her, she thinks – as if this were not schedule enough. This is what abroad is like, she reminds herself, and this is why she avoids it: the consuming rigmarole of finding somewhere to eat, getting to an address, using a bus or a metro or even a taxi. What adventure is there in having to think so long and so hard about eating dinner or getting home? Where is Thomas's poetry, she demands savagely, in this confusion of streets, misunderstandings, this aloneness, this distraction?

She goes to the brasserie. Eating her *sole normande* she feels a sweet nostalgia for that night, her first in Paris, when she sat here with Daniel and his blonde, artificial girlfriend. Was it only three days ago? Three days since she had a normal conversation, with someone she knew, three days since she laughed or even spoke normally. How near Tommy seemed to her then: a mere telephone call away, a simple, inspired enquiry.

She arrives at Strasbourg Saint-Denis at a quarter to eight. She has never seen the area after dark; it looks at once more seductive and more theatening, now that the legitimate marketplace commerce has been shifted away and there are only the riotous windows of cafés and bars, one after the other. During the day there are still the authentic inhabitants of the *quartier*, the old ladies shopping for cheaper cuts of meat, the Africans selling rugs. In the evenings, at Strasbourg Saint-Denis, the honest dirt less visible, a new crowd takes over. The people who come here do so in search of pleasure, and the pleasures to be had here are dubious.

In the event she finds Pierre's café almost straightaway, and realises at once that it is the scummiest, the lowest of all the low and scummy cafés along this fallen stretch of the boulevard. Here the men grin openly over her. Several local whores sit over steak and chips and tea with lemon. Imogen folds herself onto a banquette, orders a coffee, in passable French now, and settles down to wait for Pierre.

At twenty to nine he is not there. By this stage she has also consumed two beers and is feeling rather light-headed. Downstairs from the main room of the café are lavatories and a payphone. An Arab girl is talking into the phone, screaming in her thick North African accent. From the lavatory Imogen can still hear her, the spitting, staccato phrases. When she emerges from the washroom the girl glances at her with total lack of interest, this stream of invective all the time issuing from her mouth, her intonation so marked that she seems to be saying the same phrase over and over again. What if Pierre should arrive while she is waiting down here? She feels sick with frustration as the Arab girl pushes another handful of coins into the payphone without, apparently, drawing breath. Finally the girl slams down the receiver and a clatter of unused change is ejected from the phone. She mutters something at Imogen and starts off up the stairs.

Imogen calls Pierre. Two rings, and then the answering machine starts up.

By twenty-five past nine a host of colourful, frowsy and variously tipsy people have come and gone. Desperately she orders another beer. From the initial stir caused by her striking entrance and the indifference succeeding it, a palpable amusement has now set in, and there is no longer any doubt in her mind that she is being subjected to a conscious and willed humiliation. But why should Pierre, why should anyone want to humiliate her like this, force her for an hour and a half to sit drinking beers in a whores' café in a red-light district of Paris, waiting for a man? Who could derive satisfaction from it? And how, how could they be so sure that she would not just up and leave after half an hour?

There is a burst of raucous female laughter. She looks up. Pierre is standing in the doorway, smiling broadly, looking around the room, almost as if he were sniffing the air like some young deer in the winter forest. He has a leather jacket slung over one shoulder. He sees her, inclines his head ironically. Naturally he does not offer an apology nor explains why he has made her wait so long. Besides, she knows why, and he knows she knows: there is a tacit admission of the fact in the way he orders more drinks for them and in the way she does not protest.

'I thought you weren't coming,' she begins harshly.

He smiles, does not even bother to challenge the untruth. 'You have eaten?' he asks. He raises his glass to hers: '*Santé.*'

He really is the perfect gigolo, she tells herself, down to the third-rate Hollywood politeness, the clichéd Italianate looks, the smile, the solicitude, the final melodramatic touch of virile brutality in the leather jacket. Even his after-shave is too strong.

He watches her thinking all this. 'You really despise me?' he asks softly.

'Why did you lie to me?'

'Lie to you?'

'When you said you didn't know who Paul was.'

'Paul? Who is this?'

'The man who wrote the letters.'

'What makes you so sure I know him?' He waves his carton of cigarettes at her. 'What do you know about me? It seems to me – excuse me – that I am more than generous with my time, it seems to me that I am doing all I can to help you.'

'Do you know what they've done with Thomas?'

'"They"?'

'Has something terrible happened to him? I have to know.'

'"They"?' he repeats, as if handling the word to check its weight, gauge its value, determine its authenticity. 'Are we *really* in a spy movie?' Slowly, theatrically, he takes out a cigarette, lights it, blows blue smoke into the air above their heads. Then he inhales deeply, looks just as deeply into her eyes, and smiles. 'It is true that I did not tell you everything at once. I didn't lie to you. I simply did not tell you. I did not know how to. And I did not know what help I could give you. With the letters – oh, that was different, not so important, anyone could have done that. I did not want to raise up your hopes too high. I cannot lead you to Thomas. I cannot tell you where Thomas is now, I did not know him so well.'

Then he talks about the Thomas he knew. 'I met him a year ago, it is not important where. We became – I suppose you could call it – friends.' Thomas whose life in those days was not so very distant from the life she could have imagined for him, doing his practice during the day, going to classes at the Conservatoire, meeting fellow students for coffee, going to twice-weekly French courses at the Alliance Française. Eating in student restaurants, attending free lunchtime concerts in churches on Sundays, inviting friends over for tea. They would go down to the record department in FNAC and buy cassettes. Sometimes there would be a party and Thomas would help with preparing the salads or making sangria. He had a girlfriend, very nice, very clever, Véronique. There was absolutely nothing remarkable about his life: the typical life of a young English student in France.

'So what changed?' asks Imogen, darkly suspicious, for his tale is filled with phrases such as 'when I met him' and 'at that time', as if their very meeting were the cause of such a sea-change within Thomas, for all that Pierre keeps stressing 'I did not know him well.' And there is the question, also, of what this most conventional of music students might find so fascinating in the company of a twenty-year-old half-Italian pretty-boy not interested in music nor, it seems, in anything much beyond the gel on his hair and the fit of his shirt.

'I cannot tell you so much,' says Pierre, looking round the bar. Catching his eye, the hennaed *patronne* beams back, pleased. She knows him. 'I've told you already. He started suddenly to have different friends.

He wasn't so much with the conservatoire people. It's normal; they were very boring, those people. It was Thierry who found him, Thierry who introduced him to me. But at the same time I think Thomas started to meet some much more important people, this Paul you are so interested in, for example, but also, through him, some very powerful people, older people. This Paul: I don't know quite what he is, some big man in the music world I suppose. Whatever he is, a terrible person I think. He was mixed up in all kinds of things. And his friends, well . . . I don't know, but I think there were some very important people, musicians of course but others also . . . I was worried for Thomas.'

'Why? Why? Why were you worried?'

Pierre shrugs. 'I knew a little bit about these people. Not so much. Enough not to trust them.' He looks across at her quite directly. 'What are you afraid of?'

It is like two days before when he said, so disarming: 'You're upset.' Suddenly all her fear comes rushing over her, the fear she has refused to acknowledge since that first day when she telephoned and telephoned. 'Everyone tells me, "Don't be scared", and everything everyone tells me is so frightening. I just want to find my son, that's all I want, I just want to hear he's all right. I want to hear his voice . . .' She is aware that her own voice is too loud, here, for this bar, for this company. She looks up, but the faces turned towards her only aggravate her hysteria, her three days old, haggard and unvented hysteria. 'I just want to find my son, that's all I want, it's not so much. Or just to know where he is, just to hear his voice, to know he's all right. Everyone says don't worry, and then they tell me things . . . I just want to find my son . . .'

Her voice is shrill in the hushed bar. Pierre stands up, as it were sweeps her out of her seat – 'We go from here, I think' – somehow by mutual agreement fixes the bill with the *patronne*, and then they are standing on the drizzly pavement outside, she crying abundantly, now only from shame and from relief at having found someone to cry to, he with his arms around her and Italian reassurances whispered into her hair.

Suddenly she sniffs, pulls away from him, puts a hand to her hair. 'I'm all right now,' she says, very English. 'Please understand, these last few days . . .'

They are standing in the rue Saint-Denis, just within the reach of the lights of the café. Shadows push past them out of the dark. Behind them is all the hectic activity of the boulevard. It is a rainy spring evening and quite cold. Pierre does not touch her, but he smiles at her, really, and in this second he is very beautiful. 'I do not require any explanation, you know . . .' He pulls out a handkerchief from the pocket of his leather jacket and respectfully offers it to her.

Overcome, covering her eyes with it, she says: 'I don't know what hit me back there . . .' They walk along the boulevard. He takes her arm, smiles at her again. Clichés frivolously crowd her mind: 'My vile seducer,' she thinks, though at this moment he looks anything but vile, with his clustering eyelashes and his expensive forelock of hair trained to flick over his eyes and soften, from one moment to the next, that dancing-boy's boldness into boyish charm. And it is altogether possible for her to see the cliché and still be overcome, as in fact it is only in speech and writing that clichés detract from what they represent, while the visual totems of popular imagination gain force through familiarity, such that this gigolo's belt and brylcreemed hair, the biker's cap and leather jacket, the cabaret singer's suspenders and the whore's Sadeian heels have acquired a lodging in the mind and conjury over the flesh as potent and dreadful as those Crucifixions and Pietàs that wait on a thousand street corners, touted by the Church, mother of all fetishes.

Now they are in the Avenue de l'Opéra. Above them is the gaudy, scarcely believable façade of the opera house, so at odds with the sleek, smug angles and perspectives which surround it. Cars stream past, but the human traffic here is thin, miserable. They turn right into a dark street of airline offices and discreet business concerns with elaborately international names. A few youths hang around on street corners in front of oddly forbidding doorways which, Pierre is quick to inform her, are the entrances to exclusive and specialised nightclubs.

The boys walk up and down with a slow, ungainly deliberation. They are all in their late teens or early twenties, their hair cut expensively and often coloured, their clothes – leather jackets, bright shirts unbuttoned – fresh and standardised. Some of them wear jewellery – square, heavy, and slightly ostentatious. Among them, now that he goes up to talk to them, Pierre does not look so extraordinary, for what is common to all of them is that same smile he gave her a moment ago, achingly beautiful and quite menacing, which, like the white wide smile demanded of air hostesses or fashion models, is as much a part of their professional equipment as it is an expression of amusement or joy. They are just like ordinary teenage boys, she thinks. When first she pictured to herself a male whore, three days ago, the image was of some fantastic Babylonian creature, dripping with effeminate iniquity. It has not occurred to her that the pose they adopt conforms not to their own limited notion of sexual attractiveness so much as to the fixed and slender confines of imagination of the entranced men who hunt them out.

Pierre is talking to a few of them and makes no attempt to introduce or even acknowledge Imogen. His voice is deeper when he speaks French, rough with cigarettes. Then he takes her arm with humiliating gallantry and they walk on. He indicates a doorway, dark blue with a tiny shuttered window. 'That,' he says, 'is a club for rich old men . . .'

She says: 'Are those people friends of yours? What were you talking about?'

His smile grows broader as he feigns, and feigns obviously, shock. 'Oh, you wouldn't want to know that. It's not very nice, what we talk about.'

'Were you talking about Tommy?'

The smile fades even though his mouth does not change; he speaks through his teeth as his hand closes very tightly and painfully on her arm. 'They are friends of mine, yes, I suppose they are. But they are a mess – drugs, and so on. I used to come here, I don't any more. Thomas also.'

'What do you mean? What on earth would Thomas be doing here?' She stops, shakes his hand off her arm, the better to think clearly.

'What I say. Thomas used to come here also. He was like them –' and he jerks his head backwards in the direction of the boys.

She stops, stares at him in amazement. 'But,' she says, 'he didn't need money. I always gave him plenty of money.'

Pierre laughs now with genuine amusement, throws back his head and laughs, resting his hand against a wall. Then they resume walking. He bends towards her conspiratorially as they walk, turning his head so that it brushes her hair, and she notices that for all his cigarettes his breath is astonishingly sweet, as if honeyed. In spite of her suspicion of him she is grateful for this solicitude. 'I think all this is a shock for you maybe,' he says. 'Maybe I shouldn't have told you like this, maybe it's stupid of me. You look so sad. Let's go somewhere where we can talk a bit, yes?' Already he is steering her with practised and almost imperceptible pressure into a tiny side-street.

'If you tell me something about Thomas,' she says. 'I have to know. I'm sure you can tell me something. If it's money you want, I can give you money.'

He says lightly: 'Oh, it's not money.' He adds: 'I am finished with all that.' They enter a bar, yellow-lit and quite unremarkable. There is a juke box and five empty tables, and a pinball machine being played over and over by the same scrofulous boy. Three men sit at the bar, and near them a woman in fake leopard-skin trousers and a long leather coat hanging open. Her long blonde-ish hair falls down her back. She is talking with agitation at the fat, bespectacled barman who polishes glasses and sometimes listens: as she talks she stabs her cigarette into the air.

Pierre leads Imogen to a table. 'You see that girl?' he says with delight. 'She is a man.' He laughs. 'Yes, it is incredible. But this is Paris.'

The barman hovers towards their table and Pierre orders so rapidly that Imogen will have no idea what it is they are going to drink. She sits there with her hands clasped in front of her, and Pierre clasps his own hands around hers. 'First, let's talk about you,' he says in a soothing voice, as to a terrified or fractious child.

'Why?' she says. 'What is there to talk about? Why talk about me for God's sake?'

'Hush,' he says. 'Don't be nervous. There's no reason to be nervous. I am not a monster, am I?' He pulls a sudden monster face at her, and in spite of herself she laughs. 'You see? I've made you laugh. I can make you laugh. You must not be afraid of me. You want me to help you, isn't that it? Well, it's good, it's very good. Because I want to help you. You're so sad. I don't want you to be so sad. So we'll talk about you.' He releases her hands, to her unexpected disappointment, and lights a cigarette. The barman silently sets down two small glasses.

'What's this?' Imogen demands. 'I didn't ask for this.'

'It's cognac,' he says. 'The best French. You're in Paris now. You know, you cannot drink tea in a Paris bar!' He laughs at his own joke and at her confusion, then he is all seriousness again. 'So let's talk about you. After all, you know so much about me already, and I know hardly anything about you. So I must just use my imagination, from the little bits of information I hear, and from what I see when I look at you. What do I see? I see that you are not happy.'

She tastes the brandy, sets down her glass. 'That's not true,' she offers. 'I am perfectly happy. Of course, leaving out of account this business with Tommy . . .'

'Now, you know, I think you are not being very honest there.' The very fact of his leaning towards her is somehow persuasive. 'Let me tell you what I see. You are there in that big house in England, a very beautiful house, so many rooms, all full of paintings and furniture, carpets and curtains. In that house you are there alone. Oh, there is your husband, of course, but I think you do not love your husband so much anymore.' She has an instinct to interrupt him, but a deeper craving to know how much he knows. She watches his very dark eyes. 'You married him a long time ago, there were many reasons, you married him for security, but that security cost you so much, no? So, you are alone in this big, beautiful house, in England, with this husband whom you do not love, but who adores you. And the more he adores you, the more you hate him, no? Am I not right in what I see?'

And if I do not agree with you, she thinks, if I do not play this game, will your every confidence about Thomas be withdrawn? She says steadily: 'Go on.'

'You have your children, and of course –' he smiles '– of course you love them. But they are not always at home. So much of the time they are not there, and you are alone in this big house, with your husband. Sometimes you dream of a lover, young and hard and beautiful, to make you feel young again . . .'

'That's not true,' she says, sincerely irritated. 'I've never had a lover, I've never wanted a lover.'

Pierre shrugs his shoulders, at ease, absolutely not disconcerted. 'So? I am wrong. It is only a guess. I only tell you what I imagine. I have a right to imagine.' He nods almost imperceptibly to the barman, who will arrive with two more brandies, and she will drink it as Pierre talks on. 'Why do you deny what you know to be true?' he says at last, his hand reaching across for hers. 'You think maybe I am exaggerating, you think I am a foolish, a romantic boy — '

'No, I don't,' says Imogen, summoning up the last of her combative animosity. 'No, I don't. I think you're a lousy lying gigolo, that's all.'

He slams his fist down on the table with such unexpected violence that the glasses tremble. But even as she starts away from him the smile slips back into place across his face and he says: '*Soit*. I am a lousy lying gigolo. But I am a lying gigolo who wants to help you. Why should I do that?'

'How should I know?' returns Imogen. 'You're too clever for me.'

Pierre looks down. 'Thomas did not tell me that you were so beautiful,' he says. His words sound improvised, as if he has slipped for a moment from some closely scripted character. She glances up in surprise: it is also the first time he has volunteered information about her son. He excuses himself rather briskly and makes his way to the lavatory. In his absence she drinks, watching the extraordinary process of her own hand closing on her own glass.

But now they are in another bar, a kind of dance hall. It is very late. 'When the bars close there are always other bars,' Pierre explains. The waiter sits and smokes with two customers. A man is playing old songs on a piano, a middle-aged couple is dancing in the exact centre of the floor, simply turning in slow circles. There are hardly any other customers. 'You are so lonely,' Pierre is saying now, and his accent, at first charming, then irritating, has ended by being mesmeric. 'So lonely and so beautiful. It is not right that someone so beautiful should be so lonely.'

'Why do you say these things to me?' she says. 'I'm not beautiful, I'm forty-seven. And if I'm lonely, it's because I want my son back.' Vaguely she is aware of the futility of arguing with him. For an hour now, or two, he has talked to her about herself, about her life in England that he can know nothing about, her youth, her aspirations, skilfully sidestepping all her attempts to draw information from him. In return he has flattered her, has stroked her hair from her forehead, has kissed her hand, and she has accepted all this gallantry with the humiliating sensation that everyone, the customers, the barmen, even down to that drunken transvestite in the other bar, has been laughing in merry collusion with the boy opposite her. But an enormous lassitude and loneliness keeps her from leaving, and soon Thomas is no longer more than a pretext: tomorrow, tomorrow she can deal with Thomas, the truth will wait, it always can. She is conscious even of a note of coquetry in her voice as she repeats: 'I'm not beautiful . . .'

Finally he leads her out into the streets, empty of people. It must be very late. 'Don't worry, I live not far from here.'

Now they are running through streets wet with a heavy shower of rain that came while they sat in the bar. The same streets, it seems, that they walked through only an hour or so before, but the crowd has gone, the doors are closed and the lights extinguished. Before the entrances to clubs, cinemas, cafés there are huge dustbins and crates of rubbish.

He holds her by the hand and pulls her along. After the choked, overheated bar it is exhilarating to run like this in the rainy air, hear her heels clatter against the pavement. Then she feels the alcohol stirring inside her, begins to feel sick and dizzy, she stumbles and almost falls. 'I can't run any more,' she says, pulling at his arm.

He looks at her sideways, disdainfully. They are at the top of a long flight of stone steps. Simply to look at them makes her feel sick. Below them is a little park with an iron fence around it, beyond it an avenue with the yellow lights of a line of taxis. 'We go down there,' he says.

'Really, I mean it,' she says, pulling away and leaning her forehead against the wet wrought-iron railing, 'I think I ought to sit here a while. Really,' she says, holding onto the railing, 'I can't go any further.' He takes her hand, presses the palm to his mouth, looking into her face as he does so. Then he pulls her up towards him, picks her up roughly from the sidewalk where she crouches, her arms around his shoulders, her legs hanging, doll-like, over his arm. She is looking up at the sky suddenly, from this boy's arms. He begins to walk down the steps. 'What are you doing?' she laughs in her fear. 'Are you mad?' But she daren't struggle lest he stumble and fall. The staircase is very long. The clear night sky, emptied of rain, begins to swim above her and she fixes her eyes on his throat. There is nothing else she can do. When at last they reach the foot of the steps he sets her down.

'Better now?' he asks her.

They walk on in silence, not touching. When he crosses from one pavement to the other she has to follow, when he turns right she turns right. They are in an area where the pavements are narrow and every window shuttered. Even on the boulevard now there is scarcely any movement. They arrive at the crossroads where Pierre spoke to his friends and said: 'Thomas used to come here.' But the boys are no longer there. He stops in front of a building, taps in the door-code, stands back politely as she steps into the courtyard. She knows she is doing something very wrong. In the hallway are huge gilt-framed mirrors and some fantastic pieces of Grecian statuary set on fake pedestals. 'There is no lift,' he tells her, 'but I live on the second floor only.'

As he opens the door to the apartment he puts a warning finger to his lips, points her through into a large and high-ceilinged room, and tells her to wait. She hears him open another door, speaking softly and urgently, hears another voice reply, no more than a murmur, hears Pierre speaking once more with a kind of pressing tenderness such as he never, in amongst all his compliments and gallantries of this evening, could have mustered for her. Then a moment later, with a wide smile on his face and two glasses in his hands, he is there in the doorway.

He sets down the glasses, switches off the overhead light, turns on a small tablelamp with the inevitable blue lightbulb. Moving like a dancer, he crosses the room to the hi-fi unit and presses a switch: it is the second act of *Tosca*, the music uncoils from the machine as if it were waiting there for this very purpose. Days later she will recall this music, how it sounds alternately, through her drunken fatigue or the pantomine of the next hour, like an exquisite prayer of devotion and like the bawling of a demented woman.

He sits her down on the large mattress. The room seems huge and sparsely furnished. There are a few framed theatre posters and a great mirror on the wall with a black shawl thrown across one corner. Shirts, underwear lie over the bare floor. Around the mattress is an amazing assortment of magazines, pages of letters, overflowing ashtrays, dirty glasses and mugs. She looks up at the chilly stuccoed ceiling of this formerly elegant apartment in the onetime heart of bourgeois Paris. A black and white cat is lying on a table in one corner of the room, watching her.

For want of something better to say, she says: 'Is that cat yours?'

'Why no,' he says, as if it is the most natural thing in the world to have somebody else's cat lying and blinking in one's apartment, master of all it surveys.

Pierre hands her a glass of red wine: it is only as she takes it that she realises how her hand and indeed her whole body is trembling. While he throws his jacket over a chair she tries to remember what is happening at this moment in the opera, but other happenings, other operas, crowd in on her memory. And somehow she is acutely, forebodingly conscious of the presence of that someone across the hallway: 'You share this flat? You have a flatmate?'

He half turns to her, his glass dangling between thumb and middle finger. 'It's just a friend who's staying here for the night. He has nowhere else to go. Like you.'

He sits cross-legged on the floor beside her. '*Santé*,' he says, and touches her glass with his own. She cannot think of anything to say, and he does not even bother to make conversation, so confident is he of the mesmeric power of his physical presence. Indeed he sighs, almost bored, running his fingers through his black hair. At some point he sets down his glass, stands up, begins to undress. His body, uncovered by such degrees, is so beautiful, it is like one more affliction she has to bear, for what is her beauty and the beauty of painting and music, compared to this?

He comes towards her, naked, and undresses her firmly. Firmly he takes her shoulders and pulls her down, all the time murmuring Italian words to her. His fingers pass through her hair, searching out and finally releasing the Chinese comb. She is crying now, her head on his shoulder. Perhaps a half hour later his body shifts from over hers, he gets up, leaves her, returns a moment later with a tall glass of water. He watches her drink it down in one, like a thirsty child. Then, squatting in front of her, balancing on his toes, his legs wide apart, he holds up for examination the apple he has brought from the kitchen, splits it with a little knife, gives one half to her and begins to eat the other. Fascinated, she too eats. The digital clock says 3.42. She lies back, shivering, and he covers her body first with the sheet, then with the blanket.

She wakes at first light. Through the window she sees solidifying the grey outlines of other windows, other rooftops. She is alone, curled up at one edge of the mattress with the sheets and covers doubled unevenly over her wretched body. It is the cold that wakes her. The room looks smaller now and dirtier, as if abandoned weeks ago. She listens for sounds, voices, before daring to move, but the apartment is empty, she can hear it. The events and faces of the night crowd in on her; she pushes them away in the immediate necessity of rising from this terrible bed, crossing this high, glacial room, recollecting, gathering up the scattered clothes and possessions as if they were the peeled layers of her senses. She stands for a moment, her hand resting on the back of the single chair, while her head swims and the pain thuds and the insidious nausea stirs inside her: the first hangover in ten, in fifteen years. Her body, so long disdained, so long confined by the dictates of her will, is going into revolt. As confronting a tailing doppelgänger glimpsed for years out of the corner of one's eye and never before acknowledged, she stands there, stunned within the sudden revelation of her own flesh, sense, appetite: *this*, then, I have been carrying around with me all this time? She catches sight of herself in the huge mirror, stares at the intruder, stares at her reflection for the first time in so many years.

She finds the bathroom. The washbasin and glass shelf above it are poignantly littered with toothbrushes, rings, empty cologne sprays, tubes of skin creams, used razors. She fills a tooth mug with water and drinks it all down. She feels increasingly nauseous, anxious to leave the apartment and yet dreading the street, and before the street the courtyard, and before the courtyard the stairs. As she crosses the hallway of the apartment she passes a wide double door, the same door through which Pierre spoke so softly and so tenderly the night before. She looks up at it. Who was it there in the other room, as she cried her drunken tears, as she let herself be undressed by the practised, nonchalant hands of the prostitute, as she clung to his moonlit, marmoreal body?

With sudden decisiveness she pushes open the door. The bed, narrow and institutional, is neatly made. No sign of an occupant.

She negotiates the staircase. The early morning is astonishingly, pitilessly cold. There are occasional cars. She goes north to the boulevard, its cinemas, theatres, restaurants. Nothing is open. On the pavement she sees unbelievable quantities of rubbish where the night before there were still the sleek and intimidating entrances to exclusive and secretive clubs. There is something shameful about being up at this hour. As she walks, the citizens of Paris, after their long night of revelry, sleep the sleep of respectable burghers, behind closed curtains and in shuttered rooms, dreaming of the day past and the day to come, as if they had never even guessed what fate awaited them, nor known the extent of a minute's reprieve.

All the young men

There are always such mornings in Paris, mornings of waking to a sour stomach in the early light of someone else's apartment. Sometimes it's possible to escape while the other sleeps on, to collect one's clothes strewn over the floor or thrown across the backs of chairs, to get in and out of the bathroom silently – silence being the crucial thing. And there are those encounters in the bathroom mirror, your pallor, the red-eyed want of sleep, as you fumble among someone else's toothbrushes and bottles. But often it isn't possible to get away so easily. As you reach for your coat the other stretches, yawns, blinks, works a smile. Then comes the dull, faltering recognition, the sudden modesty at a nakedness no longer under cover of darkness or alcholic indulgence, the reluctant offer of breakfast, always refused, the obligatory exchange of telephone numbers, and as often as not, a shameful afterthought, the names forgotten from the evening before. And of course we will see each other again . . . Kissing goodbye or not, and then the embarrassment of asking where exactly you are in Paris, what's the nearest metro station, how to get there. Outside in the unfamiliar street it is usually raining, you stumble through the cold and into an early café, there in your disco or party clothes drinking a *crème* at the counter among the inhabitants of the *quartier* on their way to the seven o'clock shift, attempting to recall with a kind of nagging masochistic precision for the truth how it was that you met that person last night, and how it was that once again you took that taxi and ended up in that strange bedroom on the other side of the city. And so home, exhausted, your own grey flat, a couple of aspirins, a telephone call to cancel an appointment or report sick at work, then some kind of sleep until noon.

At least she does not have to face the receptionist girl of previous days. A young man sits at the desk and pays her no attention whatsoever as she walks past. Her room is dismal at this hour of the morning. She takes the aspirin and sits on her bed, wondering what to do next. What were her plans? Should she fortify herself with some breakfast? Her stomach churns at the thought. Cold and twitchy, she goes to the bathroom and drinks another glass of water. *You're so beautiful, he never told me you were so beautiful.* As she stands at the sink, watching herself drink, forcing it down, the nausea rises with such incredible suddenness that she almost passes out. The next few minutes are spent crouched over the lavatory bowl as wave after wave of sickness passes over her and is exhausted. Afterwards she lies for some time on the bathroom tiles, the sweat turning cold on her forehead, and is bleakly astonished by the thought of how similar her posture and feeling is to that of last night as she lay beside Pierre, his lovemaking over. And as her mind scratches on and on for more details, she finds that from the hallucinatory sequence of bar after bar, of the boy's face opposite her, of his building, his room, the thing she can best remember is this feeling of sick cold and solitude as she lay there in the dark beside Pierre. Finally, slowly, she stands, kicks off her shoes, goes to her bed, pulls the blankets tight around her neck. In time her trembling subsides, the pain in her head dulls, and she is on the point of falling asleep when all of a sudden she remembers her appointment with Paul.

It should not be supposed at this point that what Imogen is feeling is desperation. Far from it. Unconsciously she has always measured her success in proportion to the sacrifices she has been required to make, for which it is normal that she should endure frustration, suffer discomfort, be met with hostility, ingratitude, and incomprehension. She never expects nor seeks immediate satisfaction for herself, and has always viewed the desire for it in others as suspect. She is a stranger to happiness in the usual sense of the word and does not understand people who pursue it. Happiness, for her, consists in a few brief moments of a lifetime, some unspeakable and unsharable communion with Art, or the exhausted realisation of all her strivings and sacrifices in the form of a particularly beautiful performance or gratifying competition result by one of her children. And, solitary prophet, she is far from wishing happiness on her children either, or at least any other conception of happiness than her own. Why should Tommy, why should Vicky, want to be *happy*, think they should be *happy*? Aren't they there for something more important? Boyfriends, girlfriends, holidays, parties – these are all very well for other people's children, and she tolerates them in her own as the necessary evils of adolescence; but actually to *want* them?

Instinctively, she believes what Diane told her, that Paul could not harm Thomas. Whatever else the man may have done, whatever fear instilled in her son, whatever sick relationship attempted, somehow she believes that Paul could not actually harm him. Why? It is not just the intuition that Diane is sincere, although this plays a part. No: it is Paul's stature that counts for her. And while despising the man she is already half in awe of the personage, a personage whose name she first heard three days ago. She remembers Vicky's comment: 'Everyone's heard of him'; Madame di Biasi's pronouncement: 'He takes only the very best'; Diane's hyperbole: 'the artistic conscience of his generation'. In her secret heart, for example, she is more kindly disposed towards Paul than towards Fiorenza di Biasi and her sweet put-downs. Her anxieties of the past weeks have been mitigated, even as her troubles have been increased, by what she has learned. And it is Paul, the fact of Paul, his celebrity, and more, his undeniable and so nearly annihilated presence waiting for her there in that hotel dining room, which fixes the whole affair on a different plane, elevated beyond the mere adolescent gesture or undergraduate caprice she feared it might just be. She feels disgust, yes, but her disgust is offset by a weird pride, and the result of this contradiction is a curiosity as for some fabulous monster, revolting in its individual parts and yet inspiring pity and wonder at its solitary and terrible grandeur.

One of the hotel attendants escorts her into the dining room. He inclines his head to indicate the table where she will find the great man. Paul is at this moment engaged in an altercation with the waiter, and though his voice is restrained in deference to the prevailing expensive hush of the room, he chops at the air with his hand. The waiter is nodding, nodding.

He has kept on his big overcoat, inside which he seems to huddle. He looks cold and beaten-about, he looks quite like a man who might recently have swallowed an overdose. He looks his age (which, Imogen remembers, is also her age). But he does not look bad. In front of him on the snowy cloth there is a cup of coffee and a cognac. This shocks her: a cognac at midday. Then she remembers that this is a strong, big man, no frail artist, no Chopin swooning consumptively over the keyboard, but a healthy, volatile professional punishing himself from airport lounge to recording studio to hotel room, and enjoying such worldly pleasures as time allows: good food, fine brandy. Until a few days ago.

But he is spectacular even in his fall. He seems to fill more space, seems to be more physically present than anyone else in the room. His gestures speak while his voice, even lowered, commands. His thick grey hair is steely, aristocratic; his eyes unnaturally expressive. Imogen thinks suddenly of Milton's ruined archangel. Paul Delamarche, hoisted into lonely glory by the mountain of his talent, plummeted by an unnatural passion for Imogen's son.

The waiter departs and Paul stares for a moment into his brandy. Then he looks up and sees her. Slowly, laboriously, he rises to his feet as she crosses to his table.

They greet each other uncertainly. Seated once more, Paul takes out a cigarette and lights it. She notices that his hand is shaking and that the flame dances around the end of the cigarette. A waiter approaches and Imogen asks for a coffee.

'Now that I've met you at last . . .' (At last! Three days!) 'Now that I've met you at last,' says Imogen, 'I can't find anything to say to you.'

'I feel the same, oh yes.' His accent is strong, pleasant, not so much French as warmly and generally Mediterranean. They scan each other's faces for a moment. He says: 'It's strange. I simply assumed you would look like Thomas.'

'Do you know where he is?'

'Dear madame,' he says heavily, 'if I did, do you think I should have woken up in a hospital bed?'

But it is not melodrama she wants, it is information. 'What did you want to tell me?'

'I wanted to see you because I was curious. I wanted to see the boy's mother. I wanted to see if you were as I imagined you to be.'

'Did he talk about me? What did he say?' The terrifying question.

Paul gives a small, ironic laugh. 'Nothing. He didn't talk about you at all. And God knows, we talked.' He takes a drink of brandy. 'God knows we did. And he never talked about you. If that isn't enough to fire a person's curiosity, I don't know what is.'

Imogen stares into the lonely ruins of his eyes; the intelligence.

'I saw him last perhaps a month ago. He came to the studio for a lesson. Supposedly for a lesson. He wasn't interested. I asked him what was wrong. He wouldn't sit down, he just wandered around the studio picking things up and putting them down, bits of music, ornaments. Going over to look out of the window. He said nothing was wrong, he couldn't concentrate, that was all. Then he said suddenly that he didn't know if the piano was what he should be doing. I didn't take it seriously, I thought it was just one more – how can I say it? – one more Thomasism. There were always so many! I told him not to be so stupid and asked him if he intended to work or if he had come just to waste my time. Then I saw that he was quite serious. I became angry, I began shouting at him. But it never did any good, shouting at him. He just watched me, said nothing, as I became more and more angry. He waited for me to finish. Then he picked up his jacket and went. He wasn't there more than perhaps fifteen minutes.' He tells the story in a bored way, lifting his eyebrows ironically, turning down the corner of his mouth, as if it were an occupational hazard for him, all in a day's work. Only when he stops does his face seem to sag.

'He interested me, at the beginning. He was different from the others, more intelligent. More difficult to teach in that respect. He was the only one who asked always "Why?" The others, they accepted without question. Because I am who I am . . . who I was. Thomas would ask me why. It was a good lesson. I stopped believing in my own infallibility. But that was only the first thing I stopped believing in.

'I wanted him to be great. I wanted to make a great artist of my pupil. Oh, a lot of it was vanity, of course. Most teaching is nine-tenths egocentricity, you'll find. But I wanted it for him, too. And remember: *he* sought *me* out, not I him, whatever anyone will tell you to the contrary. It was a challenge to me. But then the more I became interested in him, and the more I tried to help him, the less he cared. Listen. Once I invited him to dinner in my house. My wife Diane was not there. It was planned to be a very special dinner. You see I wanted to present Thomas to some friends of mine, people very important in the musical world, very influential. They were people who could have given him –' he spreads his arms as if in an attempt to illustrate '– immeasurable help if they had liked him.' His hands fall back onto the table. 'Other young pianists would have to wait years for the opportunity to meet just one such. And, in addition, these were wonderful, intelligent, entertaining people. And he did not come. Thomas did not come. It was eight o'clock, it was half past eight. I telephoned to his apartment; someone else answered the phone, he did not know where Thomas was. Oh, I tried to make myself believe all manner of things: an accident, a misunderstanding over the date. But inside I knew. He was punishing me. Punishing me for the trouble I took for him, for the help I offered him. The next morning he telephoned. He said he had not come, he did not know why, he had no excuse, there was no reason. Can you imagine what that did to me? That dinner had been Calvary for me, the most terrible evening of my life. And he did not apologise, even. Can you understand what that did to me?

'And that was only the beginning. After that he went out of his way to humiliate me. If we made an appointment anywhere he would simply not come, I would wait in some damn café for hours. If he said he would telephone I could be sure he would not telephone. He would offer excuses knowing that I would know that they were lies – he'd been in cinemas that had closed down, at classes that had been cancelled, visiting friends I knew were abroad. In his lessons he would play deliberately badly, would "forget" everything I had told him the week before. Or he would arrive with some terrible friend of his, that so-called actor, for example, or even someone he had run into at a party the night before. Anyone. In my house. Bringing them to me. I took him to Italy, hoping that the change might give us a chance to work things out. After two days he simply disappeared with a group of Danish students and only turned up twenty-four hours later.'

She feels a faint distaste, not only at the content of his stories but at his self-dramatisation also, his apparent enjoyment, his eagerness to tell her all, that she know all. Why is he lacerating himself like this in front of me? she wonders. Is he really so far gone? And then he falls silent again, and she looks at him, at the eyes misted over, at the face tired and heavy with shame, and she thinks: yes, he really is so far gone. 'Why did you stand it so long? If you knew he wanted to humiliate you?'

Again that strained smile. 'All it took,' he says, 'all it took was one little person who didn't believe in me. That was what I couldn't live with.'

The great man. 'Did you – did you love him?' she asks. He says nothing, he watches the smoke rising from his cigarette. On an impulse she opens her bag and flourishes the letters at him. 'What about *these*?'

He looks up in astonishment and takes them from her, squints at them for a moment, then draws out his glasses from an inner pocket and flicks them open. She watches his face darken yet further, her accusing stare is fixed in readiness, but it fades on her own face as he reads on and on. At last he looks up. 'Where did you find these?'

'They were on his desk, in his flat.' And without knowing quite why, she naggingly recalls her feeling of something wrong, something disturbing, at the moment she found Paul's postcard in the mailbox at Strasbourg Saint-Denis.

'But — ' He really seems at a loss for words. Quickly shuffling through the pages now, he examines them with ever-increasing bafflement, she watching him with equal impatience. Then he lays down the sheets, removes his glasses, and his hand reaches out vaguely for his cognac. 'I don't understand,' he says. 'I don't understand. I didn't write this.'

'What do you mean?' she exclaims. 'I told you, I found them — '

'Oh, yes, yes,' he says hurriedly. 'They're my letters, certainly. The words. My God, I'd know them. But this isn't my handwriting.'

And that is it, of course: what has been troubling her these last few days, the unconscious itch. That handwriting, large and urgently leaning, so pregnantly, so fortuitously identified by Pierre as 'the handwriting of a madman', bears nothing in common with Paul's messy, preoccupied scrawl. Paul's hand is trembling now, is fluttering over the sheets of paper which bear the perfect copies of the letters he wrote to Thomas. He begins to say something.

But in the Crillon, even in the Crillon, so far removed from the year-long World's Fair of the Place de la Concorde outside, even here one is not protected from one's own celebrity, and suddenly there is an admirer at their table, a little bespectacled middle-aged man, smiling with wonder at the renowned musician.

'. . . eum, Monsieur Delamarche, eum, Monsieur Delamarche . . .' He speaks in hushed tones, as if in church. '*Je vous prie de m'excuser, j'ai toujours été parmi vos . . .*'

With one sudden furious movement of the edge of

his hand Paul sends the brandy glass flying against the wall. The brandy leaps out, the glass shatters. They stare up at the stain dripping its tears down the costly wallpaper.

A waiter materialises beside them. The poor small man's lower lip is trembling, he looks around as if for some escape. What little noise there was in the dining room has been silenced, and though few of these excellent guests stare openly, they are waiting for some outcome to the scene.

Imogen looks down from the tears forming behind the little man's spectacles. He seems to shiver, once, then walks back stiffly to join his companion. Paul is staring at his hand with a kind of amazement, and it is left to the waiter to recast the incident – *rien qu'un accident, monsieur, ça se produit tous les jours* – drop a napkin over the sopping tablecloth, and summon an inferior to brush up the broken glass. The hush over the other tables relaxes until it becomes once more genuine.

'My nerves,' mutters Paul. 'The idiot, bothering us like that.' But it is obvious that he is the most shaken. He breathes deeply, shudders in his coat, looks up at the waiter. '*Encore un cognac, s'il vous plait.*' The waiter's lips compress a fraction between the wisdom of serving more drink to so volatile a client and the deference owing to such a renowned personage.

'*Oui, monsieur,*' he says at last.

Paul half-closes his eyes. 'I'm sorry about that,' he says to Imogen. 'That . . . exhibition. My nerves.' He passes his tongue over his lips. He tries to regain himself. 'These letters, I don't understand. You found them where?'

'In Tommy's flat, on his desk.'

Paul thinks for a moment. Then a slow, bitter smile spreads itself over his face. 'Don't you find,' he says, 'that Thomas has gone to considerable trouble in making sure that you find the key to Bluebeard's chamber?' She stares at him. 'What is so surprising?' he says, openly mocking now.

'Your way of putting it. And only the other day — '

'Yes?'

'Only the other day Véronique – Tommy's girlfriend – called it Pandora's box.'

Paul essays a vague gesture. 'Pandora's box, Bluebeard's chamber, it's all the same' – the same Freudian nightmare.

'Then where are the originals of these letters?' asks Imogen.

'God knows. Oh, I suppose they will turn up, at the appropriate time. Like Thomas himself. At the appropriate time.'

He stares ahead. He no longer seems interested in her presence there, no longer seems to have anything to say to her, seems to be retreating into his vast loneliness wherein he can turn over, can weigh his heavy knowledge in peace. She is losing him and with him that knowledge of his. 'Please,' she says. 'There is one thing I have to know. Did you and Thomas ever — ?'

He looks down into the formations of grain at the bottom of his coffee cup. 'No,' he says. 'No. No, I never did.'

She wonders if he is lying, wonders for no better reason than he has proverbially declined to meet her eye as he answers, when she should know that there are a dozen reasons why one might look away from one's interrogator in all sincerity: shame, defeat, or simply to avoid the pain in the other's face.

'But you wanted to,' she says. 'You tried.'

Now he looks up at her, his head on one side, his eyes heavy. 'What do *you* think?'

Imogen grips the edge of the table. It is with great effort that she manages to say: 'You disgust me.' Great effort, for it is not in fact disgust that she feels at all.

This seems to recall him to the present. 'Why?' Almost casually, with purely academic curiosity he asks it: 'Why? That's why we're both here, after all, isn't it? We both love the boy. How else do you expect me to love him?'

Turning her face away from the dining room, she begins to cry silent tears.

'One little person who didn't believe in me,' Paul the damned is repeating softly, tenderly. 'That was all it took. Please, tell him that from me when you find him, would you?'

When finally she arrives back at the hotel it is already late in the afternoon. She has been wandering in Paris. She has bought books she does not want, fabrics she does not need. 'What does madame require?' 'Does this not please madame?' She arrives back at the hotel. 'Madame Holm,' says the voice of the receptionist in the same plaintive tone as the hawkers along the Boulevard de Rochechouart, 'Madame Holm, there is a letter for you.'

It is not a letter, in fact, simply a Polaroid photograph stuffed into an envelope. In the centre is Paul, flanked by Thomas and Pierre. Some sort of party is in progress. Paul has his mouth wide open, but it is difficult to tell whether he is laughing or whether he is simply in the act of recounting some terribly hilarious story. His arm, that illustrious arm which has enfolded and enthralled so many millions of concert-goers, is stretched around the shoulder of Thomas who, for the camera, is looking ironically down into his empty glass.

On the other side is Pierre, facing the camera, ready for the photo, his over-eager lips pouted as if for some special kiss. It does not take too much imagination to establish a relationship between the three of them. They all three seem to be having a very good time.

'I'm sorry, who brought this letter?' asks Imogen.

'Oh, I really don't know, madame.'

'And you don't know when?'

'It must have been sometime this morning, madame, when I was not working. It was in your box, madame, that is all I know. If you want to know more, madame, you will have to wait until tomorrow, when . . .'

Imogen does not wish to know more.

She goes to the phone and calls Pierre from there. There is no answer. She calls Daniel. Likewise. She calls Véronique, likewise, Tommy himself, likewise. Then she calls Pierre again. And again. Over and over she receives the same sentence: *Pierre n'est pas là pour l'instant, mais si vous voulez laissez un message . . .'*

Propped up on the payphone is the photograph. It is by an almost intellectual and quite difficult process that she identifies the individual in the picture as Tommy, the Tommy who would spend the long long afternoons of the Easter holidays practising away in the large and airy music room in their house in Haslemere, with the sun streaming in on him and on the polished black of the Bechstein grand she had persuaded her husband to acquire, while next door in the kitchen she might be found buttering mounds and mounds of potted meat sandwiches for the vast feast to take place that evening in honour of Damien's thirteenth birthday. After a time Tommy had wandered through into the kitchen, rather aimlessly, before helping himself to some coffee which stood still hot on the stove. Spreading clingfilm over the plates of sandwiches Imogen said: 'It's sounding quite good, the Scarlatti,' and Tommy smiled, not bothering to reply, for what did Imogen understand about music anyway?

After an early dinner in the Café de Milan, not really a dinner at all, just some fish thing and half a bottle of wine, a token, something for her to do, she goes out into Paris. The boulevard is growing dark, the yellow lamps chasing away the remnants of daylight. The boulevard is as usual filled with people on their way to or from somewhere, and the few dispossessed regulars who hang around in amusement arcades or in front of bars too expensive for them to enter. She has called Pierre twice, each time a voice has answered in French from which language it has refused to budge or understand anything else. It is imperative that she see Pierre, imperative that he provide some explanation for that photograph, so deliberate, so provocative. If this is a challenge, she tells herself, she will rise to the challenge.

The evening wind is blowing rubbish about in little whirlwinds, bits of paper, polystyrene fast-food dishes. She drinks a pichet of wine in a neon café called Plaza. It is a way of passing the time. Then she drinks another. For the thought of confronting Pierre sober is too intimidiating. On the opposite side of the road she sees a snake of people already lining up in their weekend rags outside some kind of jazz-club, spivs in sharp suits and molls in shimmery blouses and gravity-defying coiffures, up from the suburbs for a night to remember. She tries to imagine Tommy, blinking in the spectral blue light of some disco, manoeuvring his way from the bar to the dancefloor. Or rapping on the door of some club, waiting nonchalantly as the tiny window is drawn back and the unseen eyes examine him, or unplugging the phone at five-thirty in the morning and slipping into bed and sleeping until noon after a night of God knows what excesses, God knows.

She leaves the boulevard and turns down a street as far as the crossroads where Pierre talked to those friends of his who were standing there and afterwards told her as if it were the most normal thing in the world, 'Thomas used to come here too.' It is still only half past nine and there are not too many of them there, and though in their outer aspect and attitude, in their black leather trousers and jackets, their chains and their heavy sadistic jewellery, they seem quite familiar, quite interchangeable with the boys of the other night, it is possible that they are all quite new and would not even know who Pierre was were she able to ask them. Certainly none of them seem to recognise her, they just go on talking as if it is really not worth their effort to break off a conversation and look interested when there is only a woman walking down the street.

After three or four tries she finds Pierre's house: she recognises it by the weird statuary and mirror arrangement in the entrance hall which lends a bourgeois prestige to this otherwise quite dismal building. Her mind somewhat befuddled by the wine, she cannot remember which floor he lives on and so examines the mailboxes in the hall. She remembers his name: Saporito. Saporito. There is no Saporito in the building, it appears; but when she sees the name Delamarche inscribed on one mailbox, she knows where to go.

The door is opened by a very large black man with a moustache, wearing a fantastic oriental dressing-gown with vast sleeves. She just catches sight of a much slighter, much more ordinary boy of twenty disappearing into another room. 'I've come to find Pierre,' she says in English at once. 'Is he at home?'

The negro, who is really quite handsome in a very

huge and overpowering way, grins to reveal a startling number of teeth. He leans on the edge of the door for a moment. 'And who might you be?' he enquires in cornmush deep-south American.

'I'm a friend of Pierre's,' she replies rapidly, at which he takes away his massive arm from the door and admits her into the apartment. Instinctively she looks at the other room of the night before. The double doors are wide open, there are astonishing amounts of clothes littered over the bed, the lights are on, and somewhere inside the room a tape deck is playing an old blues number.

The negro leads her through to and sits her down in the large room where she spent the night with Pierre. The mattress is now folded over and covered with a spread and pushed against the wall to approximate a sofa, and the discreet lamps make the room look almost cosy. The cat is lying in exactly the same position as before, blinking malevolently at their impudent intrusion into the room.

The negro puts a large whisky into her hand. The ice rattles against the sides of the glass as she holds it. Meanwhile the other young man, with very short brown hair, dressed in jeans and a T-shirt, pops his head around the door, just to see what is going on.

The negro settles hugely into a chair just opposite her and sips his own drink. She manages finally to ask: 'Who are you?'

'Why,' he says, 'my name's Carson.'

It sounds like a joke or made-up name to her. 'And are *you* a friend of Pierre's?'

'Everybody is looking for Pierre today,' he says, lolling at great ease in the chair. 'I reckon as how Pierre has always been a cute little thing, but I doubt as he has ever had so many visitors nor people seeking him on the phone. His popularity is hitting new heights, I guess. Why, only one quarter hour ago sure as I sit here was two gentlemen asking if we'd had hide nor hair of his whereabouts. Unfortunately I wasn't able to informate them, seeing as how I've not set eyes on Pierre twenty-four hours or more. But I reckon as how they had different reasons for seeking out Pierre than your good self, seeing as how the both of them was in uniform and carrying police ID. Now, what kind of call two gentlemen of the law got with our Pierre? What kind of mess he got himself into?' The man spreads himself out yet further over the limited space of his chair. 'Well, I reckon as how wherever he is, he's getting himself well looked after. Don't know anybody like Pierre for finding the warmest place to lay his head, just like that ole cat there.'

Imogen sits forward in her seat. 'You know him then. Do you know Thomas Holm?'

'No, I can't say as I do,' says the negro with intense satisfaction. 'Who might he be? He a friend of Pierre's?'

'Yes,' says Imogen, downing half the whisky in one. 'He's my son.'

The man chuckles richly at this. 'Why then, I reckon as how you'd be doing yourself a favour to ask this son of yours where you might locate Pierre's whereabouts, because sure as hell I can't put you wise.'

'I would,' says Imogen, looking sadly into her whisky. 'But I don't know where he is. I'm trying to find him.'

'Sure as hell a lot of people disappearing these days, it's like some epidemic.'

'And he –' Imogen waves her glass vaguely in the direction of the other young man who has just departed. 'Does he know anything?'

Again the negro chuckles. 'Doubt it. He don't even

understand French, let alone English.' He installs his feet on the coffee table for a minute. Then suddenly he says: 'Are you sure you all right? You're looking a bit sick, a bit green, if I may say.'

'I'm quite all right, quite all right,' says Imogen, somehow replacing the whisky glass without spillage on the table before her. Even so, she allows herself to be laid down on the couch for a while by the negro, assisted by the young and silent man who comes hurrying through to help him. 'I feel a bit ill, that's all,' she murmurs.

She lies there for a while and the boy brings her water to drink and after ten minutes she feels ravaged but somewhat better. 'I have to go now,' she says, swinging her legs to the floor.

The negro opens wide his huge encompassing arms. 'You don't want to stay here? You, a friend of Pierre's —'

Outside it has started to rain a little and this does her good. She makes her way back along the boulevard, gaining a little confidence with each step. It is imperative that she find Pierre and hear his explanation. Still she feels somewhat shaky but it is unthinkable that she should give up her search at this hour.

She walks on to Strasbourg Saint-Denis. Perhaps she will find Pierre in the café where he made her wait so long the other evening. It is worth a try. And even as her mind clears she realises that she wants Pierre for himself, and not for anything he can tell her, anything he can give her. It is for himself she wants him now.

She is at the junction of Strasbourg Saint-Denis, the red-light district of Paris. The activity here is tremendous. She remembers Pierre, his lashes, his thick thick hair. Looking around her she sees the many many men hovering around, the girls posed in their doorways. This is where I belong, she tells herself. Then, hard on the heels of that thought: What, are you mad?

She pushes her way into the yellow lights of the Café La Lune. The faces swim before her, turning to her, she takes no notice of them. There is a young man with black thick hair and a leather jacket, she recognises him simply from the beautiful back of his neck. He is talking to some terrifically painted girl who is laughing, laughing at his words. She sighs. 'Pierre,' she calls out, moving slowly across the bar, her coat steamy with rain. 'Pierre!' But when the boy turns round, too late, it is not Pierre, his mean and handsome face is quite different from Pierre's. And the girl, too, looks up at her with quite unconcealed hostility.

Now it is raining heavily in the street. She doesn't know where to go. Where is Tommy, the author of all her trouble? Where is Pierre? People surge out at her, out of the darkness. Somewhere ahead of her there is a fight going on. Some prostitutes are clawing into a man who has attacked one of their colleagues. Imogen begins to run, her heels kicking up the puddles of rain. A man bars her way suddenly, murmurs something in French. She pushes past him. Imogen faces the street, its sharp particularised predicament. Behind her, laughter breaks out.

Bluebeard's chamber, Pandora's box

The party in Thomas's apartment which Daniel attended was officially in the nature of a housewarming, although Thomas had already been living there for four months. He was sitting with Véronique one evening, watching her study, watching her small head bent over a textbook, when 'Let's have a party,' he suddenly said. Véronique put a finger between the two pages of her book, looked at him for a moment, and said: 'Yes, we could, why not?' Immediately Thomas took a sheet of paper and they began to compile an extensive list of possible guests, Thomas putting his head first on one side, then on the other, at each suggestion, for the mix of people was important, their diversity, and because – his mother's son in this freakish respect - he viewed such an event from the artist's angle, although unlike his mother he was concerned less with ensuring an aesthetic unity to the party than with achieving an entertaining and quite private satisfaction for himself.

Although a lot of thought went into the guest list, superficially the party conformed to the stereotypical party organised by relatively penniless students or young people in Paris at that time, in so far as with few frills the maximum number of people were brought together in the minimum amount of space, encouraged to make the maximum amount of noise and drink the maximum number of drinks so that 'at least everyone will go home with the illusion that they had a good time,' as Thomas explained this strategy to Véronique. So a handful of crackers, peanuts and chips were bought in alongside institutional quantities of wine and vodka, the ordinary lightbulbs were replaced with red ones 'for atmosphere', the carpet was rolled up and stuffed into the kitchen along with the apartment's few breakables, Thomas stuck a notice above the mailboxes of the building apologising in advance for any disturbance, and at about half past nine the first guests trickled in.

There were people from the Conservatoire, people from Véronique's college, people from the fashion magazine which Véronique sometimes worked for, people from Tommy's early days in the bookshop. Then there was a sprinkling of what Véronique and others were already beginning to call 'Thomas's new friends', in particular the actor-barman Thierry and his colleague, plus a photographic model called Francesca who claimed to be Italian and whom Thomas professed to adore, and a short, blonde, insolently sexy girl of Russian birth and Israeli citizenship who claimed to be writing a doctoral thesis in history. When next day Thomas and Véronique conducted the post-mortem of the party they were able to calculate that eleven separate European nations had been represented, and all the five continents of the world. In addition there were several uninvited guests: three 'friends' of Thierry who worked in a boutique; Thomas's neighbour, a wild-eyed, wild-haired Polish woman dance teacher, who came to protest about the noise and stayed to augment it; and three unidentified young people from no-one knew where but who came bearing such generous quantities of hashish that nobody felt inclined to complain.

There was a lot of coming and going, a lot of drinking and dancing, surprisingly much considering how small the apartment was and how difficult it was, by moments, to move. Somewhere around midnight there was a mixer shortage and Véronique volunteered to go off to the local late Arab store if Daniel agreed to go with her, this giving them a chance to talk. Thomas was looking hugely amused by his own party. When they returned with their purchases they found him seated on the sofa watching the whole carnival with a vacant-eyed, almost silly smile, and Véronique realised that he was quite drunk. She took him down into the street and walked him round and round in the night air. She left at about two, by which time Thomas was revived and dancing with the Israeli historian. The party broke up at around four and some people slept the night on the floor, while others huddled in the kitchen chatting until the first metro.

There was absolutely nothing remarkable about this party beyond the fact that it was Thomas's first, and in his own apartment, and that it happened when Thomas's life was undergoing some sort of transition, even if at the time this meant simply the shedding of certain old habits and certain old priorities and certain old friends. It provided an opportunity for some of the old circle to meet some of the new, and in so doing to realise – as was the case with Véronique, for example – that there *was* a new, and that they were not necessarily part of it. She was not alone, later, in regarding this evening as a turning-point, nor in seeing something other than pure accident in his choosing this precise moment to celebrate his occupancy of the apartment at Strasbourg Saint-Denis.

Imogen: 'How can he bear to live here?' – seeing the dirt, the gloom, the decrepitude of the building. But Thomas was so happy when he found this apartment, his first real apartment, so happy with the crazy neighbours, with the sinister *quartier*, with the boulangerie across the road where, finally weaving home at past six in the morning, he would buy the day's first croissants, with the bar round the corner which stayed open all night and where it was a regular guessing-game which of the locals downing measures of wine or Calvados were coming from bed or heading there. And this room, its peeling walls, its floor adrift with dust, this was the room where he had invited friends and strangers alike, where he had first gone to bed with Véronique, where he had first had a party; where he had first sat with conservatoire acquaintances until five in the morning listening to Mahler, where he had first tried drugs, where he first had his plan to deceive his mother and go off to Spain; where he had first brought a strange man, just any man, for the experience. All the people who had passed through this apartment! The drug-dealing girlfriend of Thierry's who, evicted from her room and nervy about the police, had spent a week on his floor and then one fine day upped and gone taking all the teaspoons in the apartment with her. The millionaire opera director Paul introduced him to. Paul himself had been here, though not so often. A sixteen-year-old

Hungarian backpacker encountered at four in the morning once when Tommy was heading back from a vodka-crazed evening at Thierry's, and just picked up there in the street, for the boy had nowhere to sleep and Thomas felt reckless. Small, squalid, starved of sunlight, in a fetid ramshackle building in an increasingly violent corner of the city: it would be difficult to explain Tommy's attachment to this apartment or guess at his real regret when the time came to abandon it.

Imogen sits there, crouches there almost, on Tommy's bed, in the vanishing afternoon. She has been sitting there for half an hour, just watching the gloom intensify, the walls and furniture greying over. She is waiting: for what? For some inspiration, some supernatural intelligence to emanate from Tommy's things, Tommy's books, such as guides those mediums called in to trace vanished children? She looks around at his possessions, and they do not betray him, the objects he left behind him, carefully, just to show he was there.

She is crying. Once again, helplessly, she flicks open Tommy's address book, looks at all those names, tries to remember one in particular he might have mentioned. But Tommy has never talked about friends in particular, has always talked about friends as 'friends': '. . . over at a friend's place', 'went to dinner with some French friends', 'a friend whose family lives in the country', And even when she asked a second time about that girl's voice on his answering machine he said: 'Oh, she's just a friend.'

And what does he mean by 'friends' anyway? What degree of intimacy does he imply with the word? She has never asked about these 'friends'. Was Véronique a 'friend'? How would he designate Daniel, Pierre, Paul himself?

Imogen does not have friends, which statement

should not be understood as pathetically as it might sound but rather as something equivalent to saying she does not smoke, having simply not chosen what for others is variously pleasurable, necessary, or dangerous. An orphan, she has no family behind her. Her husband she can no longer bring herself to speak to civilly, and the people who come to the house are his friends primarily. She has a horror of casual acquaintances but does not allow herself time enough to develop anything deeper. Her life is family and solitude, family and precious solitude. And her children – they are everything, but they are not friends. She doesn't even know if they like her, has never really cared. And it is entirely without self-pity, but with a shock at the peculiarity of her position, that she realises she doesn't have a friend in the world, she only has children.

Today she has lost one more illusion.

The last entry in Tommy's diary was for April 13th: *2 pm, Hotel Bouvy*. No name, nothing else. Enlisting the help of the unhelpful receptionist of her own hotel she located the place, far over on the Left Bank. An ordinary hotel, not so big, in a quiet street: rather like her own in fact. Hardly the place one would arrange a meeting without particular reason for doing so. She went up to the desk and waited as two old people, Germans from the sound of them, chose and paid for some postcards. At least the bespectacled woman behind the desk was speaking to them in English. Imogen waited for the two Germans to move off.

'Is there any way of knowing,' she asked, 'I mean, do you have any way of telling me – who was staying in this hotel on a particular day?' Only then did she remember to add the apologetic preamble: 'I'm sorry, I know this request must sound strange . . .'

'Of course,' said the woman. 'If you have the name, or even the room number would be sufficient . . .'

'I'm afraid I don't have either,' said Imogen. 'I just want to know who was staying in this hotel on April 13th of this year.'

'May I ask why?' said the woman, girding up her *froideur*.

'I am trying to find my son. He seems to have disappeared.'

'And what is his name?'

Imogen closed her eyes with the effort of remaining reasonable in the face of enquiries which were, in fact, quite reasonable. 'It won't help you,' she said. 'He wasn't staying at the hotel. I think perhaps he came here to meet somebody. Please. I'm very worried.'

The woman sighed, spread out her hands with that air of offended exasperation which even the most naturally cheerful and obliging of French people cultivate as a professional *atout* and which eventually becomes quite effortless. 'Madame,' she said, 'this is Paris. People move on, particularly young people. They move on all the time.'

Then she looked into Imogen's face, and something she saw there, the tiredness, the unhappiness, caused her own face to soften. 'Let's see if I can find the register for that week. The 13th you said it was? Maybe I can help you.'

She came back with some huge, white, stiff sheets of paper. Turning one at right angles on the desk between them she ran a finger down one column: 'This is the date in question. Is there anything here . . . ?'

None of the names were familiar to Imogen, nor for the 12th, nor the 11th. Warming to her own helpfulness, the woman said: 'Perhaps if we look at the week before.' She pulled out another sheet from underneath the first. 'You understand, if it was a long stay perhaps we would not transfer the name from the one sheet to the next, we would simply mark the room as still occupied.'

Together they looked down the columns, 10th, 9th, 8th, Imogen already so sure of being defeated, of being embarrassed, that she might easily have missed it. Suddenly her finger stopped. She stared at the paper. 'Ah, this was the lady you were looking for?'

'Yes,' said Imogen, 'yes, that's her. Do you remember her?'

'Oh, I'm afraid not, madame, you know, these are only names . . .'

She thanked the woman for her help, unaware that the devastated expression on her face more than belied her gratitude. She walked out into the street with such a physical sense of unreality as she had experienced the few times in her life when she had drunk too much. But her head was clear enough to persist wondering, to persist imagining, what Thomas had wanted from her friend Susan that day.

The receptionist called out uncertainly after her: 'I hope you are successful in finding your son.'

The ringing phone jangles her nerves. 'Hello? Hello?'

A pause. 'Oh, is that you, Mrs Holm? Is . . . Thomas there? This is Diane Delamarche.'

The immediate disappointment. 'No, he's not here. I haven't found him.'

Diane sounds distracted. 'I see. I thought he might have turned up. That's why I called this number.' Pause. 'Have you heard from Paul?'

'No. When? I mean, I saw him yesterday . . .'

'He's not here,' says Diane, her voice very high, very

tight. 'I don't know where he is. He may try to get in touch with you. If he does . . .' She stops.

Imogen feels slightly sick. 'Is he . . . ?'

'In a bad way, yes.'

No sooner has she set down the phone than there is a knocking at the apartment door. Her immediate feeling is one of relief, but it quickly gives way to a nagging fear. After all, what does she really know about this Paul? What earthly reason does she have to trust him, to help him? A failed suicide, a hysteric (she remembers the flying glass in the hotel restaurant), violent in his anger and desperate; a man who entertains God knows what sick passion for her son and God knows what resentments against him and perhaps – who knows? – against herself. Why should he get in touch with her? 'In a bad way, *yes*.' She stands there in the hall, weak with indecision, while the light, confident rapping comes once again.

But it is only Pierre. Even as she opens her mouth in surprise he lifts a finger to his lips, inches past her into the hallway, and pushes the door shut. 'You were looking for me,' he says at last, his voice mockingly over-solicitous. 'I got your message. You see? I came for you.'

She follows him into the room. 'Where were you yesterday? I looked for you everywhere.'

'Oh yes,' he says, throwing himself across the bed, grinning up at her. 'I'm keeping out of the way at the moment. I'm in danger. There's going to be trouble.' In spite of these words his great eyes are gleaming with excitement, and, though he is as cologned as ever, there is a faint smell of sweat about him which, while not in itself unpleasant, is like a flaw in his whole immaculate set-up. For the first time she feels a catch of real physical fear at his presence.

'How did you know where to find me?'

'I call your hotel,' he says, amused, 'they tell me you aren't there. Where would you be, at the *Tour Eiffel*?' With a sudden lunge he reaches between his wide-apart legs for his carrier bag. 'I brought some beer. I don't mind a drink or two while I'm working.' Which comment she does not require him to explain. 'You join me?' She shakes her head. 'I go get an opener.'

It is almost dark in the apartment, she looks around for the light switch. She hears him in the kitchen, opening a drawer, rattling through the cutlery. He is back in a moment, tossing the bottle-opener and catching it with one hand. '*Voilà.*'

She sits on a chair opposite him. 'You certainly seem to know your way around here.'

He waits before replying to remove the cap and take a long pull of beer. Then, laying down the bottle on the table he says: 'Sure. Like a second home to me.'

She is at a loss what to do, what to say. He, on the other hand, seems to be enjoying himself hugely. 'Why did you come looking for me?' she asks at last.

He widens his eyes. 'But I thought it was you who was looking for me. That's what I was told.' He reaches out suddenly, an incredible movement, his whole body thrusting forward from the waist, his hand shooting out to touch the side of her neck. She flinches away, stares at his outstretched hand in horror. He repeats: 'That's what I was told.'

'It was that photograph. Did *you* leave that photograph at the hotel? I wanted to see you about the photograph.'

He laughs. 'Oh, photograph, photograph! What is this, another clue? You have found another clue?' He picks up the address book, flicks through it with derision. 'Here we are, Thomas's address book. More clues.

Did you find anything interesting in it? Second time around?' He tosses it back onto the sofa.

With a real effort she manages not to start crying. Finally she says levelly: 'You don't have to be so cruel.' The smile disappears from his face. He drinks some more beer. 'You know Paul Delamarche,' she says.

'Yes,' he says slowly, almost sulkily. 'Yes, I know Paul Delamarche.' He drinks some more beer. He rubs the back of his hand against his eyes and then runs his fingers through his hair. His good humour is quite gone. He takes out a cigarette. 'Yes, I know Paul Delamarche.' Looking up at her. 'OK, I'll be square with you, okay? No more fooling around.'

She watches him.

'I know Paul Delamarche, sure I do. Paul Delamarche is a pervert. Paul Delamarche is a bastard. Sure, I know him. So great, he thinks he's some kind of God. But he's not so high and mighty, going around after all the kids. Sure, I know him.'

She asks evenly: 'Do you also know that he took an overdose of sleeping tablets three nights ago and almost died?'

There is only a flicker of surprise. Then: 'Well, it wouldn't be such a bad thing. No way. A pity it didn't work. Paul Delamarche is no good. I know why he took an overdose. I know him.'

'What have you got against him?' she asks. 'What has he done?'

He swivels back round to face her. 'Listen. I told you I gonna be square with you. Listen. I told you there's going to be some trouble, that's why I'm keeping out of the way. I mean it: I'm in danger. Thomas is in danger.'

She has known it, all along she has known it. She wanted confirmation, now she has it. Tommy is in danger. 'Oh God . . .'

'You ask me have I seen Thomas. It's not safe for me to see Thomas, not safe for him to see me. I don't know where he is. But that's not important. The important thing is that in a few days – a *few days*, you listening? – it'll be over. Just a few days more.'

'What kind of danger is he in?'

Pierre looks down. 'It's not nice. I don't like to talk about it. But this man – Delamarche – he's not so nice. But he's not the only one, he's not even the most important one. There was a whole band of them, they had a kind of network. My God, Paul Delamarche is nothing beside some of these people. Listen. There is a bunch of crooks here in Paris. Italians and Corsicans mostly. They sell kids, I mean, on the streets, real kids, fourteen, maybe thirteen sometimes, I don't know. And not just on the streets, they have some special service with the phone; you call up, you get a girl, you get a boy, what you want. And this Paul Delamarche and maybe ten, fifteen more, he used this service, he kept paying.'

It is back, the same sick feeling of unreality. 'Go on.'

'And now the police know about it, know *something* about it. And in maybe two days' time, for Paul Delamarche and for all those other guys, it's going to come out, and they are going to be *finished*. You ask me, that's why he swallowed pills. He can't face the scandal.'

'But I still don't understand! Where does Tommy come into it? And you?'

Pierre sighs, looks at her sideways before opening another beer. 'Somewhere they got onto something, the police, not much. And somewhere they got my name. I don't know how. Maybe a guess. And they came to talk to me, said, look, we know everything, and I believed them. And before I know what's happening, I'm telling them names of these people. Delamarche and the others. And then I see from their expressions they don't know shit. But it's too late. And maybe I would have told them anyway.'

'Why?' she asks.

Pierre says in a very low voice: 'Because of what Paul Delamarche did to me.'

'Like what?' she demands harshly. 'Like giving you a flat of his to live in, perhaps?' But Pierre doesn't reply. '*What* did he do?' But Pierre only shakes his drooping head. 'And Tommy? I still don't understand.'

Pierre looks up. 'Simple,' he says. 'Paul thinks maybe it was him told the police.' He shrugs. 'Sure. Logical. Thomas knew more than anyone.'

Imogen is still thinking furiously. 'But it doesn't make sense!' she bursts out. 'What *danger* can you be in? What are you frightened of? That Paul and his friends are going to come after you? A wretched middle-aged musician who tried to kill himself only three days ago? It's impossible!'

'Oh no,' says Pierre in a quiet voice. 'Oh no, we're not worried about *them*. They're finished. It's the others we're worried about.'

And, seeing she doesn't altogether follow, he says with insulting emphasis: 'The big boys, you know? The Corsicans, Italians. The ones who run the whole thing.'

She says wildly: 'And the police! Why don't you . . . why aren't you . . . ?'

There is a heavy knocking at the door. They are both on their feet in a moment, she already moving towards the door, he clasping his hands swiftly, firmly, on her shoulders. 'Don't answer it!' he commands. She bites back tears, she is quivering, perhaps it is only thanks to his hands on her shoulders that she is upright. 'Stay calm.'

'But it might be . . .'

'Exactly.' He cuts her off through clenched teeth, his fingers tightening a little. 'Keep your voice down.' Then, more gently: 'I came to see you. You believe me, don't you?'

'I don't know!' she says.

'You *have* to believe me.'

'I don't know!' she sobs, twisting her face away from him. 'Can't I go and see? You could stay in here and . . .'

'Don't talk crazy!' he spits out. Then, gentle again: 'Please believe me. I'm Tommy's friend. Paul was never Tommy's friend.'

Another bout of knocking, heavier and more prolonged. She presses her mouth against his shoulder to stifle her crying, she is wilting, terrified, in his arms, as much resistance in her as in an unstrung marionette, as all her need of him floods into the little space between them, all her loneliness for Thomas, all the disillusionment of the past few days.

He puts his arms around her, his fingers touching, barely touching, her hair. 'Come on. Come on. It will be better. Don't be afraid. Don't make a sound. You wanted me to come, didn't you? I came to find you, didn't I?' She doesn't move. 'Didn't I?'

'Yes!' she sobs. He leads her over to the bed as the knocking continues. Someone is pummelling their fists against the door. Pierre sits them both down, his arms still round her. His lips find her cheek, her forehead. Her eyes are squeezed tight shut against his shoulder.

'Nobody will come in here. Nobody will bother us. You wanted me to come, didn't you?'

The knocking stops, and in the sudden silence that

follows she realises what he is doing to her, his hands at her throat, at her blouse. She stares at him in sheer amazement, blinks at his face a mere few inches from her own, she cannot even pull away.

She tries to find a voice. 'No. Oh please, no,' she says. 'Not here. Not here.'

But he presses her down onto her son's bed, and when she lifts up her hands to stop him brushes them away as if they were of no more consequence than lapel lint or summer insects, and all the time he is murmuring: 'But you wanted me to come for you, didn't you? You wanted me to come and I came, didn't I?'

A fresh beating at the door drives her up against him once more, in her terror, even as he undresses her, unfastens her hair, she clings to him even as he must pull away to remove his own clothes. And all the time the noise goes on, the whole apartment seems to quake with it. Only Pierre's hands are firm, his movements measured. And all she can find to say is over and over: 'Please, not here, not here.'

Later she lies there in Thomas's bed, a twitch of misery. Beside her the boy blows smoke at the ceiling. He turns his head to look at her for a moment, sort of smiles with the corners of his mouth, turns back to the ceiling. She pulls the covers over herself and then round herself, terribly cold, while he, splendidly indifferent to his nakedness now – and after all, is not this his second home? – he lies there in his warm and resilient flesh. Some time passes like that.

The telephone rings. Long afterwards Imogen will identify the whole Calvary of her coming and staying in Paris with just this sound, Thomas's telephone ringing unanswered in his apartment. At once her hand reaches out to take it, and Pierre's steel hand clamps down on her forearm. 'Leave it,' he says, smiling broadly. 'Who should disturb us at a time like this?' She looks into his face and again suffers the force of that native hypnotism of his, at the same time as his hand tightens yet further and the idea occurs to her, altogether without surprise, that he would be quite capable of breaking her arm if he deemed it necessary. As though her thought has telepathically communicated itself to him he says: 'I really wouldn't risk it, in your place.'

With his other hand he gently touches her shoulder, the shoulder of that arm to which he is already administering such indignity. And long after it has become obvious that no one is going to answer, shrilly, insistently he rings on, the one who knew she would be there.

Perfectly timed

Turning his back in misplaced and Catholic modesty, Pierre fits on his trousers and prepares his departure. With an indifferent gesture he throws her her blouse: 'Here, you better put this on, you'll catch cold.' She doesn't move to take it and sits there in the bed watching him tug at his fly. She thinks what a thug he looks now, in the aftermath of her seduction: how easily all his charms and tendernesses of a few moments before can be broken down into the various textbook aspects which form the basis of his profession. His hair, for example, falling over his eyes as he struggles with his belt: he looks very beautiful and she utterly despises him.

He sits on the edge of the bed, facing away from her, and pulls on his socks and shoes with unseemly haste.

He throws a glance over his shoulder and demands irritably: 'Are you going to stay there all night? Anyway, I'm going.'

She looks at the back of his neck, so wonderfully made, so smooth, so golden. 'I don't know what all this is about,' she says. 'I don't know why you came here. I don't know why you did this. I don't suppose you enjoyed it.' His hands, in the process of pulling tight the laces of his shoes, become utterly still, and an unseemly flush spreads over the perfect tan of his neck. 'I know I'm not going to find Thomas. I know that now. You know that too, but you've known it all along.' He does not move. 'But don't imagine you'll be making me any lonelier by walking out on me now than you did ten minutes ago.'

Still he does not move. Suddenly she sits forward and puts a hand on his shoulder, tries to bring him round to face her. 'You're crying!' she says.

'No.'

'You're crying!'

'It's my turn,' he says, looking away. 'Last time it was you, this time me. That's the way it is.' Savagely he fastens his shoes, throws his jacket over one shoulder. He repeats: 'That's the way it is.' He stands before her, pale with unspeakable anger, trembling in his need to be loved or at least well thought of: he is twenty-one years old. Then, helplessly: 'Time to go now, for me. I don't want to stay around. There's going to be plenty of trouble whatever.' He moves to the door. 'So, then – *ciao*.'

Imogen turns her face to the pillow. 'What? Oh, yes, *ciao*.'

*

The call comes through next evening, sometime after ten, as she lies on her rigid hotel bed. 'Yes, it's Diane. Yes, it's happened. I knew it would. Will you come over. Please? Now, take a cab, anything . . .'

So once more Imogen sets out for the house in Saint-Germain-en-Laye, and they sit in a salon silent with mourning. The lamps are turned low, they speak almost in whispers, as if fearful of being overheard. 'When did he do it?' she asks.

'It was about six o'clock yesterday afternoon,' says Diane. 'He threw himself in front of the train, from the railway bridge. The phone call came through maybe quarter to seven. Where were you yesterday? What were you doing then?'

'I was in Tommy's apartment,' is all the answer Imogen gives.

'Of course,' says Diane. 'He was trying to find you. Paul.'

'I know.' It was all perfectly timed, she thinks, perfectly timed so that Paul should be calling and beating at the door of Tommy's apartment as she lay in bed with the gigolo who was also Tommy's friend. Now her own complicity has been perfectly established.

The very big room is, even so, dwarfed by the grand piano. On the walls are all kinds of framed photographs, autographed mementos from friends and acquaintances. Many of the faces are recognisable to Imogen: Bernstein, Michelangeli, Shostakovich. And not only musicians, for the President of France is here, and the foremost novelist of England. Simply to look at the walls of this room is a cultural lesson. And then there are the pictures of Paul: as a child performer, alternately solemn and grinning in concert dress at twelve years old; receiving his first international prize at nineteen, gesticulating nervously with anti-climax, his hair in disarray as he faces the crowd; the maestro at thirty, explaining in a television interview what he was trying to do in his performance of the Goldberg Variations; standing on the rostrum of the Salle Pleyel with his conductor, a circlet of flowers around his neck, in sweat and tears at the end of a concert in support of the new free Romania. He was a big man, a great man.

'I read a stupid article once,' says Diane. 'Well, stupid from my point of view. Which said that if someone wants to kill themselves they'll always choose the same method. I was stupid enough to believe that article.'

'You mustn't blame yourself,' says Imogen, twisting a bracelet round and round.

'*Myself*?' says Diane with something like a laugh. 'Oh, believe me, I don't blame myself. *I* know who was responsible. *I* know that if Thomas hadn't come into our lives Paul would be sitting at that piano, rehearsing for a concert or God knows what . . .'

'That's too easy as well. That's just going to the other extreme. You can't fix the blame as easily as that for suicides. They always have to decide for themselves.'

Diane waves her glass dismissively in Imogen's direction. 'Come on: we both of us need somebody to blame. Me: Thomas. You: maybe Paul, I don't know.' They are silent for a moment. Then: 'Oh, I know. Paul was already halfway towards damnation when Thomas met him. And don't think I'm trying to exonerate Thomas. Most people are a little bit damned somewhere or other and it doesn't have to be fatal. Maybe Paul was a little nearer the edge than most. It just needed Thomas to finish him off.'

Imogen recalls how she saw him that day, sitting there, a ruined archangel. She tells herself: 'No. That's just my damned painterly imagination at work again.'

As if divining her thoughts Diane smiles and says:

'He was just a man, really, whatever he did. It must have started long before Thomas, Thomas simply speeded up the process. It was like a disease Thomas brought into his life: he showed Paul how empty his life was.' Imogen looks up swiftly as if to protest and Diane gives another, heavy, ironic smile: 'Oh, I know – we put on a good show.'

Then she tells it: 'There was another boy, maybe three years ago, another pupil of Paul's. Of course I had no idea what was going on. Then, even when I began to guess, I didn't want to know, I told myself that it was all just an aberration, it wouldn't last. Well, I waited and waited, and in the end it seemed as if my patience had paid off. The boy disappeared, and afterwards there were no more problems. No *real* problems. Until Thomas.'

'And Thomas?'

'There was never anything between them. Not like with the other boy. Oh well, God knows, I say that, even though I never knew by the end when Paul was telling the truth and when not. But somehow I believed him when he said there had never been anything with Thomas. Oh, he wanted to, Paul wanted to, Paul was besotted. He could hardly think about anything else, hardly talk about anything else. He would call up his friends, the ones who might just have been able to help Thomas: "Why don't you give Thomas a recording contract? Why don't you sign Thomas up for concerts?" They didn't know what had happened to him. I mean, I was ashamed.'

'Why did you put up with it for so long?'

Diane sighs in her great fatigue. 'I'm old-fashioned, I guess. At least, when it comes to something like marriage. You see, when I married him it was for keeps.'

A pause. 'And then?'

'And then. I don't know what kind of world it was that Thomas introduced him to. But before long there was a boy, that Italian boy, you know the one, that Paul was keeping – paying for his apartment and so on, giving him handouts, God knows what. That was hard, my God, when I found out, that was hard. I mean, Thomas was a musician, but *this* boy . . . And then of course there was blackmail, too, after a while. Not from Thomas, oh no, Thomas had moved on by then. And you must know how it is with blackmail, how it eats away at you, having to calculate your shame, put a price to your guilt. Somehow it makes it so much more tangible.' She stops to pour them each another tiny glass of cognac. It is extraordinary how graceful a hostess she is, the widow, sitting there ready with her bottle of cognac and with the story of her husband's life and so recent death.

'He was very careful. Thomas, I mean: Thomas and Paul. I saw him just that once, when I followed them to Italy. I was curious, you see. I wanted to know what he was like, this boy who had . . . who had taken up residence with us. I don't know what I expected. He was a perfectly normal boy, quite nice looking, clean, nothing so very remarkable. I saw them in that café in Verona. That was all.'

The door opens and another boy, tall, stooping, quite nice looking, nothing so very remarkable, comes in. His light brown hair is untidy and he looks to Imogen in terrible want of sleep. He has something of Paul about him, even though his face is so hollowed out and his movements so weighted with tiredness. Now Imogen can recognise the boy who climbed after Paul into the ambulance those few nights ago. He leans against the back of the sofa, blinking even in this muted light. He seems not even to notice her as he and Diane exchange a few sentences in French. Whatever she has been saying seems to reassure him, he nods weakly, essays a smile, then withdraws.

When the door is closed Diane says: 'That's Simon, Paul's son.' She looks to Imogen for a reaction. 'So you see, there isn't only me. Simon has lost his father. It was Simon who was supposed to watch over him when I wasn't here. Paul gave Simon the slip. Simon came back from the shop with Paul's cigarettes, and Paul was gone. It was Simon who had to go to the hospital to identify him.' She gazes down into her drink. 'You'll excuse me if I didn't introduce you.'

She watches her drink swim round in her glass for a moment, then is suddenly active. She takes a big framed photograph from the piano. 'Don't you think Simon looks like his father?' It is Paul aged maybe twenty. He is in concert jacket, white dress shirt, black bow tie. In spite of his professional garb he is smiling broadly, as if all this were the hugest game – he, this music, his own celebrity. Yes, in a way he looks like his son, but really it is only their youth they have in common, he looks just as much as Tommy has looked on occasion, looks even not so different from her Italian lover of the last afternoon, in those brief moments when he allowed the mask of his performance to fall.

Diane stands up. She says: 'I asked you to come because I wanted you to hear something. Someone left a message on the answering machine yesterday. Of course, I know it's Thomas, who else could it be? But I wanted you to hear it.' As she speaks she is rewinding the cassette, listening to a snatch, rewinding further. 'I never heard his voice. He never called here when I might answer the phone. If he ever left messages they were wiped off by the time I might hear them. In my own mind I'm sure, but I want you to tell me that this voice is his.'

Imogen listens to the message: it is the first time she has really listened to her son speaking French. She listens to his voice, urgent, quick, sure, that voice through which you could almost hear his smile, that voice she could identify even if it were speaking Russian or Japanese. His nearness, his so recently past and unceasingly recoverable presence in this room, fills her eyes with warm and lonely tears even as it evokes for her that whole other life of Thomas's, that foreign and incomprehensible tapestry of alliances and enmities, all woven in this strange language which he chose and which has served his stratagems and purposes for close on two years.

'What does he say?' asks Imogen when it is over.

In a bored voice Diane recites: '"I want to tell you that we won't be seeing each other for quite a while. I'm going away. Don't bother trying to find me, I don't know yet where I'll be. Maybe I'll send you my address when I get settled somewhere. I just decided it was time to move on. Given the circumstances, I'm sure you'll understand."'

'That's all?'

'That's all,' says Diane. 'God! Isn't that enough?'

Imogen covers her face with her hands. Diane says: 'Do you want to hear it again? Just to be *sure*?'

Diane says: 'I shouldn't blame you. I know what loyalty is, after all. It's not the easiest thing in the world.' She looks at the stranger in her room: 'I wish I could pity you, sincerely I wish I could. As it is, I'm too full of hate. Go. Go find that son of yours. You heard him just now. You see what he's done. It only remains for me to congratulate you – '

Imogen stands up swiftly.

' – it only remains for me to congratulate you,' pursues Diane, 'on having brought such a perfect monster into the world.' And the mother has no answer to make to this, none at all.

Once you cry

When Thomas tried to kill himself or whatever it was he was doing when he swallowed all those sleeping tablets three years ago, the headmaster allowed him to remain at the school on condition that he see a psychiatrist. This is a detail which Imogen conveniently blocked out of her memory as was her habit with all his mistakes and failures, the better to accommodate her family portrait. Though she never said as much nor even paused to acknowledge the thought, it was her instinctive attitude that psychiatrists are people paid to encourage you to say disloyal things about your parents. And in a sense she was quite right. And this is one of the reasons why Thomas jumped at the idea with such enthusiasm. As he once commented, years later in Paris, every child wants revenge on its parents, and he perhaps more than most.

However, as regards Imogen's attitude to the psychiatrist idea: in addition to her moral queasiness she failed to see the necessity for it. She had by now so far rationalised the whole affair as to have exonerated Tommy of all but the most incidental blame for his own suicide attempt: her vivid and propagandistic imagination had worked hard to people the school with a dozen malignant rivals, unhinged friends and persecuting masters, all of whom, it was quite obvious to her, had conspired to push Tommy over the edge.

It must be said in her defence, nonetheless, that in her mania for shifting the blame each time one of her children went astray she did not always exempt herself, and when for instance Tommy in his eighteenth year grew so very distant from her she unflinchingly recalled how little affection she gave him as a child for all her generosity, how willingly she substituted open-handedness for open-armedness, in her absolute terror of physical tenderness and her impatience for him to grow up and become interesting.

So Thomas went to the psychiatrist recommended by the school doctor, and for three months it was wonderful, sitting in that curtained room twice a week, every word of his listened to, even the worst, the cruellest things he could find to say. He even began to exaggerate in a kind of private contest to surpass himself, and a giddy excitement to see just how far he could go with his mother, his sister, his friends, his hatred for the piano, his sexual desires and vengeful fantasies. But in time he came to feel obscurely cheated, in time again came up against the bitter realisation that there never would be any reaction, he could go as far as he liked with impunity, it was just words in a room. Suddenly he stopped telling things to the psychiatrist, started to behave in a normal way, and the doctors and school authorities concluded that his treatment had been successful and sufficient.

Likewise Paris was wonderful for the first few weeks. He had a face which won friends easily, there was always someone who wanted to go for a drink or a film. But soon there was the loneliness of the big merciless city, the constant shifting from room to anonymous room, the swift boredom with his own kind – those international students crowding out at City Rock Café or Pizza Pino, dreary as the French kids making off to their parents' suburbs as soon as class was over. Their easy relationships, their undemanding satisfactions. He found other circles: they were better than nothing. Then there was Paul, his bitterness against Paul, the great man, the man of ideals, who yet refused to see him as he really was, who couldn't look at him squarely. Though his outward behaviour altered almost imperceptibly, more and more he took to disappearing into his own private world, just as in his childhood, those occasions when his sister Vicky would complain: 'Tommy's gone *off* again.' Now from this refuge he would still watch the people around him, the people 'close to him', and would observe with bitter, ironic satisfaction that they hadn't even noticed any change, didn't realise how absent he was. But of course you can never really disappear, never disappear completely. That was his problem. That is the predicament.

The scandal has broken, as Pierre suggested, as Paul feared, and as Thomas intended. She is sitting with Véronique on the terrace of a large brasserie in Les Halles. Véronique is translating to her from a newspaper. Their heads bend over it, Véronique in her wary sympathy, Imogen in her shattered pride.

> ... figures from the media, from the artistic world, from politics ... an extensive network of adolescent prostitution operating throughout the Paris and Ile-de-France region ... directed, it is believed, from Corsican headquarters ... adolescents, French nationals as well as immigrants from Martinique and Guadeloupe, lured into prostitution, often with drugs or threats of denunciation to the police ... names are being withheld to protect ... Police investigating the matter have refused to answer allegations that the suicide, Thursday, of internationally renowned concert pianist Paul Delamarche is in any way connected with the revelations of the Italian-born male prostitute whose testimony, earlier this week, set the enquiry in motion. The 21-year-old Naples-born youth is now under police protection, as there is reason to believe that threats have been made against his life and the lives of certain of his associates. Further revelations ...

Imogen did not expect the girl to agree to a meeting. But yes: 'Of course, I will be there in half an hour.' Perhaps the flowering scandal has placed the whole affair in a different perspective, far beyond the ragged collection of personal rancours, individual betrayals and isolated fears which, only a few days ago, it still was. Now Véronique looks up at her with those eyes full of intolerable pity. 'Shall I go on?'

'Is there anything more worth knowing?'

The girl shrugs.

'Who knows,' says Imogen. 'Maybe this was what pushed Paul Delamarche to do what he did. Knowing it was all going to come out.'

'This boy,' says Véronique. 'The Italian. The one who started it all. He was Thomas's friend, am I right?'

'A sort of friend,' says Imogen, looking out at the street. 'I met him.'

'Did he tell you any of this?' She lifts up the newspaper.

'Obliquely.'

'Poor Tommy.'

'You feel sorry for him?' demands Imogen. '*You*?' Véronique smiles away from her. Imogen continues heavily: 'Save your pity for Paul Delamarche. And for his wife. She has to live through it all still.'

'And for you?' says Véronique. 'You ask no pity for yourself?'

'I don't know. I don't know if I didn't deserve this. I could have stayed away. I need never have known anything about it. Tommy would have turned up sooner or later, when he was ready, with enough stories to set my mind at rest. I could have stayed away. He'd been trying to tell me for years that he wanted to live his life for himself. But I wanted something in return, you see. For all I'd done. You see, I gave him everything.'

Véronique says: 'Don't you think he was banking on just the fact that you wouldn't stay away?'

'Do you think he wanted revenge on me for something?'

'I don't know,' says the girl. 'If he did, he couldn't have chosen a much better way, could he?'

Imogen smiles sadly. 'What a lot can happen in two years in a foreign country.'

'*Happen*? Nothing happened. He did it all.'

And so they indulge in their fantastical and quite useless speculations as to Thomas's motives, and the morning of the day of Imogen's departure wears on, and the scandal unfolds further, ever more mordant details.

Again Véronique smiles, into her past and her very

different memories of Thomas. 'Poor Thomas,' she says again.

A waiter comes up, rather impatient. Véronique rummages in her bag and says she had better be going now.

'You amaze me,' says Imogen, referring still to the girl's pity. 'He made you so unhappy.'

'He still does,' says Véronique. 'This isn't bitterness. Maybe you can only be bitter about what someone did to you in the past. This is different. He made me unhappy for always.'

'That's what you said before.'

'Oh well, you know, it hasn't changed.'

'Anyway,' says Imogen, 'you don't seem to have been the only one – not that that's any consolation.'

'Oh I know,' says Véronique, 'I think it's a gift with him, just like playing the piano. Except maybe even more so than playing the piano.'

'You could be right there.'

The girl stands up, pulls the belt of her coat. She says suddenly: 'You're a remarkable woman, you know.'

'Yes, but Tommy's still missing,' says Imogen.

Véronique gathers up her things, smiles in a lop-sided way, then disappears into the street. 'He made me unhappy for always.' Véronique has learned what Tommy had always known, that once you cry in front of someone, it's forever. You can never forget it, the sight of them can never let you forget it. And all this, Paul and Pierre and Imogen herself in Paris, the scandal, the tragedy, has been the sound and the spectacle of Tommy trying to dash the congealed tears from his face, from a face and a skin that will not coarsen even after so much salt water.

Imogen goes into the brasserie and calls Daniel. 'Well, I didn't find him. No doubt he'll turn up when he's ready.'

'No doubt,' says the voice of the golden boy. 'I'm sorry I couldn't give you more help.'

'Oh, you did what you could. It wouldn't have made much difference anyway. If he'd wanted to be found — '

'Are you so sure he doesn't?'

'Now, fairly sure.'

'Well, I'm sorry anyway.'

'So I'm going back to England this evening. I hope you'll visit us if ever you're homeward bound yourself.'

'Well, thanks so much, but it might not be for a while. You see, Renata and I are off to Germany tomorrow morning. I got this contract suddenly, it was completely unexpected. We'll be gone at least a year. I'm sorry.'

'Don't keep saying you're sorry, please. It's we who should be sorry, Thomas and I.'

'Oh, for God's sake, don't blame yourself for anything Thomas has done.'

'He's my son. It's difficult not to. I was always ready to take the good side for myself. Why not this, too?'

'Not really. You can't hold yourself responsible for him for the rest of your life. Even if you might want to.'

'I suppose so.'

Next she calls Pierre. 'Ah, I'm very happy that you called. I wanted to say goodbye.'

'How did you know I was leaving?'

'*I'm* leaving. Someone is taking me to America. I am here to pack some things. The plane leaves this evening.'

'So does mine. I read about you in the papers. I take it you know what you're doing?'

'Of course. It is one of the reasons why I must go. It is not safe for me, here, for a while. You never found Thomas?'

'Not really, no. But I suppose you knew that already. I suppose you've known that all along. You still have nothing to tell me?'

'Is there still anything you want to know?'

'No, I suppose not.' Then she says: 'I'm surprised, you know, about the scandal and so forth. I thought it was just a story of yours.'

'Oh, it was true all right. But not the way we told it.' He sighs down the telephone with genuine regret. 'I could have warned you in the beginning. I could have told you. I almost did, that night in the bar. But you wouldn't have listened, would you?'

'No, I wouldn't. Well, goodbye then.'

'Are you sorry for what happened?'

'Please don't start. Let's just say goodbye.'

Imogen puts down the phone, stares at it in her desolation.

She goes to an Air France office and confirms her flight for this evening. It occurs to her that, for politeness' sake alone, she might well call Diane to say goodbye. But what should she say after their last conversation? Why can she not simply disappear, like Tommy and all these others?

As she passes in front of a shop of electronic items, hi-fis, televisions, a boy in a leather jacket walks straight into her. She has the impression that she has seen him somewhere before. With a smile he reaches out to steady her, his hand under her elbow. Then he turns his head towards a tiered display of televisions playing in the shop window, and she too looks, to see on six or seven screens the distraught, frightened face of Pierre, his mouth working furiously as he names names, denounces everybody. He is wearing a narrow black jacket, a white shirt, a black tie, his hair is unbrilliantined, he looks like a truant schoolboy of about sixteen. His eyes are wide with that look of absolutely justified and unblinking indignation which tomorrow will pass around the nation for bruised, abused innocence. Then the picture changes to a woman newsreader, calm and untouched in her studio. Imogen turns after the boy who so propitiously directed her attention, but he is already disappearing down the steps of the metro station.

She walks on aimlessly, now that it is all over. The time that remains between now and her departure seems ridiculous with waste and boredom. Now perhaps is the moment that she should spare a thought for that Paris – look, here are the buildings you read about, here the avenues he told you about. She stops in front of a boutique which somehow straggles onto the pavement with its stands and racks of postcards and prints and stationery. All the same, she reasons, she should not go back to England empty-handed. The boys in particular will want to see some real proof that she has been to Paris. She opens her bag: there is the photograph of Tommy at a party with his hair in his eyes, which Véronique gave her, and the photograph of Delamarche and Pierre and Tommy at that other party, and the photograph of herself smiling out of her sheer alarm when the stranger snapped her that first morning in front of Sacré-Coeur. She smiles to herself: this is hardly the kind of evidence to impress the boys. She chooses three cards, of the Place Saint-Michel, of the Moulin de la Galette, of the Opéra. Who are the people who appear on postcards, fortuitously passing before perfect views under improbably blue skies? She will show the postcards to her two youngest, and no doubt only then will observe the figures carved into the fountain at Saint-Michel or the peeling colours of the little houses in Montmartre. She steps up to the counter, the despiser of photographs, and pays for her cards.

It is past midday. The tables of the cafés and brasseries are filling up with the office workers and shop assistants of the area; they order a sandwich or a salad, a beer or a Perrier, they laugh or complain about work or home. On the tight circuit of their lives – office, café, metro, home – they pass before her, push past her with varying degrees of patience or discontent, the men in suits and ties and the other men in jeans and T-shirts, the women in blouses and jackets and the girls in sweaters and mini-skirts, the ones with wives and husbands and the ones who don't yet know with whom they'll be spending the night, the ones with children and the ones with mothers that they adore, condone, revile, forgive, forget. A couple stands up to leave, the metro disgorges fresh multitudes, the lights change and the lines of cars cross the river.

And this is when she sees her son Thomas, on the other side of the street, smiling with real serenity, his eyes bright, his hair glowing and healthy in the sun, not glancing behind him but surveying for a moment, contentedly, the apocalyptic street, and climbing out of the long, expensive car, its motor still running for him, its costly speed and smoothness still waiting for him, at once the wages and the prize of his diabolical mockery.

'What's the news from home? How's Toby?'

'Oh well, you know. Some things never change. If he gets through half of his exams it'll be as much as I could hope for.'

'And you? Are you painting?'

'Not really, no. Too many other things seem to get in the way.' Pause. 'You look quite well.'

'Of course. Of course I do. I haven't been ill. You're leaving today?'

'Yes, there's a nine-thirty flight. They managed to find me a place.'

'You were lucky.'

'Yes, I was. And what about your plans? What will you do now?'

'Oh, I'm not sure. There are all sorts of possibilities. One thing's for sure, I won't be staying around in Paris. It seems the moment for me to keep a low profile.'

'I think you're very wise.'

'I'll miss it. But there are always other places to go.' He sighs. 'Please don't be too upset about Susan. It was awful, I know, the postcard and so on. But she only did what she was told.'

'It's a strange revenge you've taken, when all I ever wanted was the best for you.'

'Yes. But you wanted it for yourself, too.'

'Here, you'd better have your passport back. Will you be needing any money?'

'No thanks. I'm well provided for. But thanks anyway.'

She says goodbye very briskly, then, without looking back, she crosses the street, and will soon be indistinguishable from that crowd of people descending into the metro.

A SUMMER TIDE

Tony Peake

'A total stranger can, in the way he looks at you, appropriate your entire life. Love at first sight, they call it. *Coup de foudre*.'

Lucy Hamilton's existence has become 'a still life'. No more than a creation by her artist husband, Charles, she is a woman whose identity is disappearing as her beauty slowly wanes. Originally an inspiration in her husband's paintings, their relations have eroded to a listless formality, and he paints in absolute privacy.

They have moved to live on an isolated island off the east coast of England, linked to the mainland only by a slim causeway, in a house owned by Charles' enigmatic and protective agent, Andre. Lucy's days are occasionally punctuated by fellow inhabitants of the sparsely populated community: the laconic Norman, the melancholy photographer Jorgen, and the hopelessly conventional Landies.

Into their frozen lives comes a stranger, a beautiful, sensual young man, whose own personality is an enigmatic secret. Suddenly Lucy's days are lit with anticipation – but darkened by the complex emotions that his presence arouses, and the relationships it causes her to reassess.

THE WATER PEOPLE

Joe Simpson

Water. It dominates all life forces. Its cycle links mountain summits and the sea, the opposite sides of a whole. Alternately destructive and creative, its properties are magical, mythical – and underestimated.

Most of us wouldn't care to think that it dominates – even dictates – our own lives. Yet the characters in this novel impel us to such a realization. Chris and Jimmy, two English mountaineers on the Himalayas; the mysterious hunter and the smiling major; the ageing grave-digger and the mourning fisherman – they are all, from snow-capped peaks to murky depths, linked by water.

An extraordinary *tour de force* of the imagination, *The Water People* is also an exhilarating tale of real adventure, of mountaineering in a place where pragmatic West meets mystical East – with surprising, amusing and terrifying results.

'Compelling and original'
Daily Mail

'Devastatingly honest'
TLS

SNAKES AND LADDERS

Penelope Farmer

Penelope Farmer's finest and most ambitious novel to date uses a multitude of techniques – diary, history and advertising copy, layered one on another – to explore the implications of an international research project into epilepsy funded by a large pharmaceutical company. This is a compelling narrative; about drugs, in myth and reality as elixirs of life and death; about drugmen as bringers of life on the one hand, salesmen on the other; about doctors as healers and scientists, in need of drug money to fund research. About a disease – epilepsy – that strikes suddenly, mimicking death and madnesss.

At the heart of the novel lies the deep but delicate relationship between Anna Kern and her neurologist husband, David, and the charismatic drug company executive, Carter Jacoman, who catalyses everyone around him into questioning their sense of self and moral value. The ladders of the game and of big businesss are there to be climbed, while the snakes represent the ambivalence of healing and decline. Who knows who in the end will be climbing, who falling?

'A sharply observed narrative of personal and medical ethics'
Sunday Telegraph

'Engrossing . . . I haven't enjoyed a novel this much in years'
Daily Mail

Her mock scientific study of the most unquantifiable factor of all [marriage] . . . is a gem'
Observer

MY HOUSE IS ON FIRE

Ariel Dorfman

Torn between the conflicting presssures of family loyalty and survival in a police state, a conscripted soldier returns home to the father who can't bear the sight of his uniform; children, playing house, incorporate into their game the sinister knock at the door in the middle of the night; a censor toys with the book he suspects might trigger the regime's collapse and in which he discovers his own role is laid out with unnerving prescience.

Set against the terrifying landscape of Pinochet's Chile, but with echoes beyond that country's borders, Ariel Dorfman's stories relate grand politics to the day-to-day existence of the people. With a genius for suspense, a great clarity and an acute sense of irony, Dorfman writes of love and betrayal, of families broken apart by hope and fear, of individuals for whom political authority and violence make private life impossible.

'Compelling'
Sunday Times

'Memorable . . . eloquent'
Literary Review

'Dorfman pares down to essentials, then twists away from the suspense he has been building up, into a new climax . . . the buoyancy and physicality and whooping beauty of the prose races along at breakneck speed, its psycho-thriller pace punctured by reversals, reflections, satires'
Financial Times

	Title	Author	Price
☐	A Summer Tide	Tony Peake	£8.99
☐	The Water People	Joe Simpson	£5.99
☐	Snakes and Ladders	Penelope Farmer	£5.99
☐	My House is on Fire	Ariel Dorfman	£5.99
☐	Fanfan	Alexandre Jardin	£8.99
☐	The Beautiful Screaming of Pigs	Damon Galgut	£5.99
☐	Betty Blue	Philippe Djian	£5.99

Abacus now offers an exciting range of quality titles by both established and new authors. All of the books in this series are available from:

Little, Brown and Company (UK) Limited.
P.O. Box 11,
Falmouth,
Cornwall TR10 9EN.

Alternatively you may fax your order to the above address. Fax No. 0326 376423.

Payments can be made as follows: cheque, postal order (payable to Little, Brown and Company) or by credit cards, Visa/Access. Do not send cash or currency. UK customers and B.F.P.O. please allow £1.00 for postage and packing for the first book, plus 50p for the second book, plus 30p for each additional book up to a maximum charge of £3.00 (7 books plus).

Overseas customers including Ireland, please allow £2.00 for the first book plus £1.00 for the second book, plus 50p for each additional book.

NAME (Block Letters) ....

....

ADDRESS ....

....

....

☐ I enclose my remittance for ____________

☐ I wish to pay by Access/Visa Card

Number ☐☐☐☐☐☐☐☐☐☐☐☐☐☐☐☐

Card Expiry Date ☐☐☐☐